I0571325

THE MINER STORIES

DESTINY: BOOK 6

S.E. McKenzie

Copyright © 2019 S.E. McKenzie
All rights reserved.
ISBN-13: 978-1-77281-058-5

DEDICATION
To all those left out in the cold.

This book is a book of Fiction.

Characters, companies, governments, places, events, are either products of the author's imagination or used fictitiously. Any resemblance to persons (living or dead), companies, governments, places and/or events, is a coincidence.

TABLE OF CONTENTS

Chapter 1

March 17th 2031, around 3:00 PM

"Sir, could you please refrain from smoking. Are you an imbecile? Riding on this hyperloop rail train is claustrophobic enough as it is. I feel all boxed in, without idiots polluting my air with second hand smoke," Bobby said.

"Son, don't call me an idiot." James replied with a finger over his lips. "I am one of the smartest men alive and I own this train. And don't forget son, if you ruffle my feathers the wrong way, I could disown you, and then where would you be?" James said.

"Dad?" Bobby asked. "Is that you? You sound like you but you don't look like you. How do I know that you are really you?" Bobby asked.

"Don't be an idiot, son, of course it is me. And for a man who has gone A.W.O.L. and might even be on the un-Tutonian black list, I would not start picking fights with strangers," James replied.

"Your disguise is really good. Are you really going to Mina with us? I thought you were going to stay behind and hang out with Christina and baby James," Bobby said.

"Doctor Knight recommended that I give Christina and the baby some space, especially if it is true that President Peel has me on his secret Blacklist. And I heard that I am being blamed for the mayhem that went on in the Buzzard Creek Tent City, last night," James said.

"Mayhem? What do you mean?" Bobby asked.

"It is nothing, just another fabrication, courteous of the fake news industry," James replied.

Are you worried about it, anyway, Dad?"

"Heavens no. I am a free man. I come and go the way I see fit. So I decided to make this trip a family event. How are you enjoying this trip so far, son? Your disguise is passable," James noted.

"I feel like a bug trapped in a steel tube floating in a vacuum, while moving at over six hundred miles an hour. I feel nauseous and dizzy. What do you mean that you think that you might be President Peel's secret Blacklist and are going to get blamed for the mayhem last night? And how do you know if the Blacklist even exists, if it is secret?" Bobby asked.

"What have I told you since you were old enough to talk?" James asked.

"To be king, you must understand Machiavellian principles or something like that," Bobby replied.

"Don't be smart with me, son. Please tell me that you didn't lose yourself in books while you were in the labor camp?" James asked.

"No, Dad, I didn't get lost in books, but I sure found peace and comfort in them," Bobby replied.

"You are King Coal's son, and if you refer to yourself as a bug again, I might just disown you," James said. You have caused enough trouble for me, this family and my enterprise as it is.

"Dad, please don't," Bobby replied.

"Now, you really are sounding bug-like. You know I am kidding. I love you son, in good times and bad times. I have always said that you must hone your inherited killer instincts to maintain your position as King Coal's son. To continue my reign as King Coal, I must maintain sole access to the Heartland's resources, and ignore the powers to be that we are leaving behind us. As King Coal, I have power to centralize all energy that fuels the engines of the industrialized world, and I have the power to turn the lights off and return my enemies to the

Stone Age. Cheap coal has given Tut Territory the competitive advantage over all nations, which is why our homeland has been great for so long. As King Coal, I should also refuse to disclose my tax returns to the public, just the way President Peel is refusing to do. It is nobody's business how much money we have or don't have. And why do you think President Peel is refusing to disclose his tax returns and so far is getting away with it?" James asked.

"Maybe under scrutiny they might discover unclaimed or disguised assets that were inherited from his father? Or maybe because he has immunity as president they will be holding evidence and indict him after his reign comes to an end. Or, maybe just because he is president of Tut Territory, making him the most powerful man in the universe, he is flaunting his power over the masses for fun. Don't you think that is why President Peel tweets his day away, because he is having fun? What does he do for fun anyway? Especially now that he is dieting?" Bobby asked.

"Exactly, and when I am president I will have immunity too. It is entirely possible that President Peel might have assets that have been falsely classified to avoid inheritance tax. Who knows, President Peel might be just refusing to share his tax returns to work everyone up, because it amuses him," James said.

"Maybe President Peel really is trying to avoid public scrutiny," Bobby suggested.

"That would be irrational wouldn't it? Whoever goes against his wishes gets fired, or is put on the secret Blacklist, that everyone knows about. Refusing to share his tax returns only invites more public scrutiny and suspicion," James said.

"Since when has President Peel ever had to think or act like an ordinary person? He might just enjoy refusing to share his tax returns because he can. Or maybe he is hiding that he isn't as rich as he says he is, or even as rich as we are," Bobby speculated.

"Or maybe he is hiding who he owes money to. Or maybe, just like you said, he wants to exercise his own authority over the lower ranks, because he is honing his own killer instinct in the hopes to be King Coal and replace me, one day. That is what human Supreme powers do, they hone in on their instincts, and then pass those intuitive instincts to their young. Once a person has been granted supreme power by the masses, he seems to be almighty, sometimes forgetting that he is still a mere mortal. He gets away with lying about his wealth, his assets, and the risk those assets are undergoing, and of course they are lying about their own intentions. On the other hand, technology, at least my technology, is more rational, more logical and does not need to lie to convince humans of anything," James replied.

"Why would President Peel be lying about getting audited, if he isn't getting audited? Are we getting audited, Dad?" Bobby asked.

"Maybe he loves to convince us and the general public, that he is right, even when he is wrong. I have transferred a big chunk of our assets to the Newman accounts, and we may not return until President Peel is booted out of office. Here is your new, international credit card," James replied as he handed Bobby a brand new black visa card with his new name, Peter Newman, on it.

"Thank you Dad," Bobby said, as he looked at his new credit card.

"And in my other hand, I have your new bank card," James said as he chuckled to himself.

"This is great, Dad," Bobby said as he placed his new cards in his wallet.

"And this, of course is your new driver's license, also with your new name and new identity on it," James said as he handed bobby his new identification which looked just like Bobby wearing his brand new disguise.

"Wow, I just need to remember my new name now," Bobby said.

"I think President Peel is on dangerous ground but I don't know what he is hiding. There must be a reason why he is refusing to share his tax returns with the public. My gut tells me that he is hiding something big. Maybe he is just flaunting his power over the general public, the way he loves to do. Who knows why he is refusing to share his tax returns. Maybe some of his capitalist cronies are not Tutonians. Maybe some of the members of his Exclusion League backers are Minese. Or maybe he is hiding evidence, which could prove that he is manipulating markets. Maybe he is hiding proof that he and his cronies are manipulating markets so that they can artificially maintain high prices, and benefit the international oligopoly of which they belong," James speculated.

"So which side are we on, Dad? Or more importantly, what side is President Peel really on? Bobby asked.

"We are on our side, and President Peel is probably on his side too, and no doubt, associating with those who tread on the line that divides oligopolies from monopolies," James said.

"Isn't that what we do too, Dad, not with construction but with coal?" Bobby asked.

"We are private citizens, President Peel pretends that he is for the people and he is holding public office, the most powerful public office on the planet. We don't have to pretend or hide that our person and family interests come first. We are not holding public office the way President Peel is. Our Big Seven Coal Group maintains control over the fuel that the engines of the world need to keep moving the global economy. We might have an oligopoly over the process of extraction, which is why we need to transport the products that we extract to market as fast as possible. We fuel the engines of the world, single handedly, without getting pulled back by anyone, especially not President Peel. We will remain Kings of Coal despite all the walls our Supreme Ruler puts in our way. We will move our brand almost as fast as lightning so that we can remain Kings of Coal as long as our bloodlines flow. This hyperloop rail network will assure that our access to coal, to trees and to the sea will be next to none. We can transport ourselves and our assets to key destinations, anywhere in the Heartland, faster than anyone else. We are the coal kings of the world. We own the fastest trans-continental hyperloop rail service on the planet. Our train will move the fuel that powers the engines of the world, faster than any other train on the planet," James shouted, excitedly.

"Dad, why are you shouting at me? What is the point having such quick access to the Heartland, if you lose your heart in the process? The problem with President Peel is that he convinces the mobs that fighting over sex and money is the right of might, and the mobs feed right into it," Bobby asked.

"Since when did you become so philosophical? Of course love and money are worth fighting for," James asked.

"Reading books helped me escape the constant hunger I endured in the work camp," Bobby explained.

"Well, don't start sound like one of those elite, dangerous intellectuals, I might have to disown you," James said.

"Dad!"

"Just kidding, son. Our blood runs thicker than water."

"Why are we leaving a warzone, to only enter into another warzone, Dad?"

"The entire world is at war, son, either officially or unofficially. President Peel, while protecting his own assets, is trying to assassinate my markets

. Ono will help us maintain our control over the Heartland, because it is in the Heartland where much of the world's wealth is still trapped in the ground. The Minese administration can only access this wealth by using the fastest and greatest technology on the planet, which I own. In exchange I get access to the greatest, untouched mineral and oil reserves on the planet, and you my son will no longer be treated like a criminal. War has always been the most brutal for the losers. We must hone our killer instincts and compete until the end, to remain king. In the end President Peel may be the Supreme Authority in the Tut Territory, but technology is the Supreme Power in the Heartland. The Supreme Authority might have the power to dictate to others but it cannot compete with technology, which is stronger, thinks faster and doesn't lie. Data can be omitted, but in the end data mining, the way Ginger used to do, picks up minute specks of information which can predict future events. And this capability gives us a competitive advantage over human management. Their primitive biases, emotions and desires are still ruling humans. The Supreme Authority can't change what is. The Supreme Authority might convince his followers that a wall is all that is needed to stop an invasion by angry foreigners, who believe that the tariffs President Peel has placed on foreign markets, many who used to be cherished allies, could starve them to death. The intellectuals of the world let themselves get lost in books and closed door debates. Ideals are fake just the true love is fake, because those standards of perfection are impossible to sustain," James said. "Kings are not afraid to kill to maintain control."

"When I was in the labor camp, all day long, I had guns pointing at me while I labored without rest and without enough to eat. I was even forced to soil my pants. I was hungry all the time, while I was held at the prison camp. When I wasn't working like a slave doing forced and hard labor in the camp, I escaped from my plight by reading books. And I wasn't the only one. It was the only way I had to mentally escape my prison, even though I was physically still a prisoner. Books helped me to detach myself from forced servitude and bondage. Books helped me to maintain my sanity. I was able to hang on to my identity and to my dreams so that one day I could regain power over my own destiny. When I am reminded of how horrible it is to live a life where I have no control over my destiny," Bobby said.

"Wake up, son. Destiny is all about the cards you were handed at birth. You flip a coin, you either get heads or tails or in the cold cruel world if you don't weigh down the coin, or rig the deck of cards somehow, your chances in life are 50-50," James said.

"Dad, when you talk to me like that, I feel like killing myself," Bobby said.

"Come on Bobby, don't be such a wussy. We rig our chances for a better life, just like anyone else would, if they had the power to do so. And look at us. The first to cross from North America, under the Bering Strait, into Eurasia, to kill myself. This is a wonderful time to be alive, son. We can live exciting lives regardless of how badly the economy crashes, back in the Tut Territory," James said.

"I know Dad, you are giving me every opportunity any son would be grateful for. I just remember the people I left behind in the camp, I actually made some friends," Bobby explained.

"You made friends?" James asked.

"I did. And I left them behind, when I went A.W.O.L. I don't ever want to be told what to do again, by a stranger holding a gun to my head. Maybe my future is hidden in the set of cards I was handed, but it is my deck of cards to play. Some of the people I met in the camp, will be worked to death, and die, alone. Some of those people are undocumented, and when they go missing, no one can even report that they are missing, because technically they don't exist. I felt so abandoned. People who said that they were friends, just abandoned me. They were all getting ahead in life, while I was left behind in the camp, to rot. The books that I managed to read, some of them were smuggled in by church groups, opened my mind to new possibilities and made me feel hopeful for my future again," Bobby explained.

"How many times have I told you that reading too many books leads to nothing more than a muddled brain and the wrong set of expectations?" James asked.

"I am not sure that you have ever told me that before," Bobby replied.

"Well I am telling you now. Thinking too hard will slow us down. We must go with the flow, relax while our hyperloop rail system outpaces our competitors in the race to the future. We have even outpaced President Peel, or should we call him the Wizard of Oz, hiding behind his Twitter machine, acting like he knows everything, when he is nothing more than a tired old man, out of touch with modern times. And what I saying is very basic, and reflects the behaviour of the greatest and most dominant beasts of the food chain. People do what they do to survive, not because it is right or wrong, but because they are wired to survive. That is a clue, son that I know all I need to know about hunger and despair. A lot more than President Peel will ever know. I didn't learn what I know by reading books, and if anything, books make people nervous, and even though they are full of words, books can make people feel empty and wordless because their brain is all muddled up. And once they have finished reading a book, they want to read another. The world would be better off without so many books. Books were made to be thrown away for a reason," James asked.

"Are you sure we are getting ahead, Dad?" Bobby asked.

"They haven't caught up to us yet, have they? We are building a great transportation system, which will move the fuels that fire up the engines of the world, faster than any competitor. We do this while lesser men are building walls to stop invaders who have the technology to fly over them and tunnel under them. President Peel is dictating a losing strategy. Closing our borders and adding punitive tariffs will only slow down movement of goods and make many products too expensive for ordinary consumers. Sure inflated prices may bring higher profits for his crony capitalists, but only temporarily and then the markets, which they manipulate will collapse. In the long term the economy will crash, and the conditions for revolution will be almost perfect, especially when desperation overpowers fear. Why should, President

Peel, in his capacity as the Supreme Authority over the Tut Territory dictate to me, the King of Coal. What happens if President Peel is suffering from some form of memory loss and his mental ability is in decline? Then what? I follow orders of a fool, who do I become?" James asked.

"A fool?" Bobby replied.

"That demagogue will not be to dictating me that is for sure. He is creating a fake emergency so that he can impose his losing strategy on the rest of us, as if we were living in a medieval age, without ability to fly over walls and tunnel underneath them," James said.

"Does honing our killer instinct mean that we become predators, and refuse to prey? Bobby asked.

"Yes, exactly and it also means that I will smoke wherever I choose. And remember son, one day you will not just inherit this train, you will be inheriting the earth and all of these tunnels, which are directly under President Peel's wall. Can you just feel the speed? It is so exciting. And we will be the first to reach the other side by riding a beautiful hyperloop rail train. What would you rather inherit son? This incredible hyperloop train or a stupid wall that anyone with imagination and means, can fly over and tunnel under?" James asked.

"You don't know how glad I am that we have seat belts in this thing, and handles to hold on to," Bobby replied. "I feel so sick. I can't see out. I feel so dizzy."

"Here have an extra barf bag. Bobby, I have never felt so free. We are leaving Pitville, and that horrible toxic black cloud behind us. All those disasters and chaos are long behind us. We will be creating a new league, which will give the Exclusion League a run for their money. The Utopian World Order, has a much better ring to it, don't you think. Before you know it we will be there. Just imagine a huge military zone, ordered and managed perfectly by Ono, for me. Ono will one day rise up the ranks to be my general," James said.

"I am glad that you have it all planned out, cause I am feeling super nauseous and a little frightened," Bobby said.

"You see that tunnel over there, son?" James said as the tunnel went by in a blur.

"Dad we must be travelling 600 miles an hour, I feel super dizzy whenever I look outside as the outside world whizzes by," Bobby said.

"I must admit son, you look green. You must develop a stomach for this way of travel. We all belong to the first family of transcontinental hyperloop train service, now. You see that tunnel son, it in particular is the most important one. That there tunnel leads to what President Peel calls his Winter Command Station. It has three bomb shelters and of course luxurious spas and golf greens and horse trails, just waiting for us. We are going to get Ono's help to acquire all the property above the tunnels that we are now digging. Some of the other tunnels are house our soldier bots and all the equipment they will be using to gain control over what is ours. President Peel has threatened us for the last time. Shutting down government. Shutting down the country. The very country we were born in as the kings of coal, and have a birthright to maintain that honor. We put so much of our money that we earn, into that huge metropolis that burns money as if it were coal; our coal. Once we win our war and President Peel himself is declared the enemy of the people and defaults his property to the new administration, we will be ruled by the winners of this war, us," James shouted, excitedly.

"Dad you are shouting again. Aren't you describing treason?" Bobby asked.

"Son, really be careful, remember who we all are now, we are the Newmans. We are a force to be reckoned with, and the Coaltonstones, the Kings of Coal, are our dear friends," James said.

"But Dad, the Coaltonstones are us, too, right? We are still a family right? Are we still the Coaltonstones too? Alex is still my brother and you are still my father?" Bobby asked.

"Of course we are still the Coaltonstones, I have transferred most of our liquid assets to the Newman accounts, so that we can start our new life in Mina in style. We can live like coal kings over there until we return to our rightful place as Coal Kings of Tut Territory," James replied.

"Wouldn't that be treasonous, Dad? President Peel always says he has no qualms of imprisoning anyone who questions his authority especially those who are questioning his fitness to be president. He calls the group who is trying to use the 25th amendment to remove him from the presidential throne, nothing more than a coup, devised to steal the presidency that he won when he was elected, fair and square," Bobby said.

"It doesn't matter what President Peel thinks. He ignores stakeholders at his peril. Going on about revolutions and coups, he might just become a victim of his own self-fulfilling prophecies and create one. While, we are in Mina, we are protected by Ono and we will reside in one of the most protected and secret military bases, not just in Mina, but on the planet. Don't forget son that the Divine Right of Coal Kings seals our place in this social order, and nothing will ever change that. We are Kings of Coal wherever we go. No one can negate our achievements," James said.

"Except President Peel," Bobby interjected.

"President Peel is gaslighting Tut Territory, and once the illusion is revealed, his bubble will be popped," James replied.

"President Peel has access to the nuclear codes. He could nuke all of us, especially if we are hanging out in Mina," James replied.

"Don't be such a wussy son. Life is a game of chess. You are either one of the pawns or the king. The king can only be safe when he is winning, and the game is over when he is captured, no matter how many chess pieces are left on the game board. We are merging with the Newman dynasty; long-time friends of Mina. We will continue with the merger until it is safe to return home. You are on leave from the penal work camp as Bobby Coaltonstone, but as Peter Newman you have always been a free man, to go wherever you choose. Under Ono's facilitation and military know-how you will enjoy every opportunity to grow as Peter Newman, so don't screw it up," James explained.

"Will Alex be with us most of the time?" Bobby asked.

"It is none of your business where Alex is or will be. And yes, Stan Junior is just as much your brother as Alex is. I made this decision quickly, but Muni Bugden verified that all of our papers are in good order and our disguises provide us all with a good fit for the social order we will find when we enter the militarized zone in Mina. And son, remember one thing don't think about it all, too much. Remember we are family of means, and our bonds as a family will never be broken. And as a family we are destined to enjoy a life as a unit, so none of us have to face the world alone. We will decide what action is appropriate to take after Ono and our crew expand and connect our tunnels under Tut's Palace of Governance. We will take back what is ours. In the meantime, we will travel like a real family. We will stay together as a real family, and bond as a real family," James said.

"Are you okay Dad?" Bobby asked.

"Of course I am okay," James replied. "President Peel just accused Jackson Green and Dianne Black of being enemies of the people and I fear for their personal safety," James said.

"I have heard you call Dianne and Jackson Fake News too." Bobby said.

"That is different son," James replied.

"Wonder who President Peel will brand as a public enemy next? Hope it isn't us," Bobby asked.

"Probably will be all of us; me, you and Alex. Though I am in no way as opinionated as Dianne and Jackson, I believe in my right to control my mind and to be free of President Peel's manipulation of my markets, so that he can be king, instead of me. I control my own mind and I make my own power by using my own killer instincts, just like my father did, and his father before him did. We are in charge of our life. All of us have the right to hang on to what is ours, handed down to us through our bloodlines, which creates our self-worth. President Peel is not who he brands himself to be, and he is probably terrified of being exposed for who he really is. Why would he be assassinating my markets with his draconian tariff policies straight from the nineteenth century, if he wasn't intending to be king of the world, and to destroy the self-worth in others to gain power over them?" James asked.

"So what are you going to do about it, Dad? Start a revolution?" Bobby asked.

"Exactly. Our riding into the future and leaving a disturbed homeland behind us, is nothing less than a revolutionary act. We must stay out of sight and out of mind, because whoever becomes a target of President Peel and the Exclusion League is doomed to lose power over their own mind and life. Dianne's questions related to President Peel's fitness for office are only questions everyone is asking. I personally think G.O.D.'s staff would never consider activating the constitutional amendment, which would determine if President Peel is actual fit for Presidential Office. My guess is that the procedure is way too complicated for those buffoons to navigate. We would be exercising the constitutional rights and duties of Tutonians, and sort of tyrannical to accuse someone of being the enemy of the people, especially my favorite broadcaster of the PPZ. We are more than just specs of sand lining a random beach by the sea. We, or at least me, have influence and so does President Peel. I might call Di a member of fake news, but I sure don't like it when President Peel does. I am a private citizen, so what I do is private and no business of the press. President Peel is in charge of public business so he should be under scrutiny at all times. And President Peel should know the difference. My trade secrets are guarded because my means and processes for production are revolutionary. Only idle speculators can be recruited as a source. These secret sources for stories about me and our family are fake and totally made up. President Peel's case, is different since he is in charge of a public institution, our country. I am in charge of a private entity. I have propriety rights, and President Peel has the right to secrecy if there is a national emergency or a security risk in revealing the classified information, but if he just makes up an emergency so that he can keep secrets from the general public, heaven help us all," James said.

"But Dad, you keep saying you hate the press and all the fake news just as much as President Peel does. Why are you are tearing up?" Bobby asked.

"Obviously the speed of this train is stirring up dust," James replied.

"I feel like tearing up too, I hate leaving our home and being dictated to," Bobby replied.

"Revolutions are not easy. We are moving ahead while the rest of the world is being pulled back. No politician or theory will destroy our position as a family. Home is where we tie our heartstrings. This train can outpace every other train on the planet. Peel can only imagine walls, assassinating markets, and vilifying the hardest working people I have ever met. Nothing, not even President Peel and his plot to assassinate my markets. We are on a journey to be the true first family to arrive wherever and whenever we wish, son. Our power to tunnel is second to none. I have always been a family man, and at this time, when our republic is closing its doors on the rest of the world, and Pitville is now in flames, we need family more than we ever did. I left just in the nick of time, Pitville is on fire today, tomorrow who knows what desperation everyday people will be facing. We cannot look back son. We are riding into the future. The loss of life is terrible and President Peel is threatening to withhold funds from the very people who are willing to rent out chain gangs of people to rake the forests of Tut Territory. These are terrible times, son, and people want a revolution and will fight all enemies of the revolutions. We are living in a time when those funds are really needed. Well they voted for him, they should have voted for me," James said not even trying to control his anger.

"I am glad we are leaving that hell hole. It could have been wonderful, but look at the place now. It looks like a paradise lost, if there ever was one," Bobby replied.

"Peel is blaming the homeless people for setting Pitville on fire, and he is blaming the Pitville for having trees and things that burn and he is blaming the hippies for hugging trees as if money was able to grow from them. When one of the community volunteers was being interviewed and tried to explain that there would be free meals for everyone so people can meet and try to put their lives together and stay strong, Peel made a face as is if the word 'free' was the four letter word everyone is being warned about. Anyway, son, I have all the special visas and travelling papers that all three of us will need, and yes, we will always be a family, especially on paper. I know they are pros and cons, but we have always operated as a family, because we are a family. We keep an eye on each other and care for each other and protect each other from the Exclusion League. And I am not going to let President Peel bully me into giving up any of my son's birthrights and weaken our bloodlines. My sons exist because I exist, and together we are shaping our family destiny and our bloodline without President Peel and his Exclusion League backers walling us in and stunting our growth," James said.

"I understand Dad, we must follow our dreams while awake, regardless if we are known as the Newmans or the Coaltonstones. I am fine with being Peter Newman, less baggage to carry around with me. I just have to remember to call Alex, Stan. I won't call you Stan though, if it is okay to call you Dad still, I would really prefer that," Bobby said.

"You would have more room in that head of yours to store important operational facts if you read less books. I expect and want you to continue calling me Dad, son," James replied. "Our papers are all in order. We going to the great land of Mina as the first transcontinental hyperloop rail riders. We are speeding through the universe so fast, no border between North America and Eurasia will ever be able to stop us," James said.

"I know this is a great adventure, on a great train, but I feel super claustrophobic and sick to my stomach. I am really glad this train is going to be really fast," Bobby said.

"Son, you are making our historical intercontinental sound so mundane. We are making our dream to be the first family of the first and greatest transcontinental hyperloop rail service to Mina and the Heartland, come true. We are what is actually happening. We are ahead of the clock, faster than time, even ahead of President Peel despite his pulling and pushing to keep us stagnated, we have prevailed and will continue to pull ourselves higher than our wildest dreams. We are not only traveling into the future, we are shaping the future to be great. We are the first family, to travel under the Bering Strait going from North America right into the Eurasia's military zone and the door to the Heartland. Ono will be meeting us at the gate," James said.

"Being in this windowless tube and going so fast is really freaking me out, Dad," Bobby said.

"Take one of these Valiums. Maybe take two," James suggested. "Then relax and feel the darkness of President Peel's exclusion league being left far behind us. We are starting all over again with what we were able to salvage. The rate things were going back there, I thought it was just a matter of time those Exclusion League backers were going to take me in for recycling, and my rights as a consumer would be reversed and I would be consumed for body parts before I was spit out into eternity. I am so glad I am out of there," James said.

"Dad, I would never let that happen to you," Bobby said.

"We are going so fast, like a speeding bullet into the future of a land where the people and their economy is underestimated by President Peel and his Exclusion League backers. Tut Island depends on Mina. The trade deficit between Tut Island and Mina is growing for a reason. Since the trade war, it now cheaper for Mina to produce goods that we need, than if we produce them ourselves. The Minese currency is devaluing and the Tutonian currency is inflating. If the Metropolis of Tut goes back to manufacturing, a lot of Tutonian products will be priced out of the market, and Peel knows this, and so does his Exclusion League backers. And when we arrive in Mina, we will be welcomed as citizens of the world. We will be treated like royalty, like the first family, and more importantly the first humans to travel in my transcontinental hyperloop rail network, under the Bearing Strait to Eurasia. Peel is not the only one with ambitions for a family dynasty," James said.

"But won't we be landing in the super-secret military zone, which is the central control of the entire Heartland? Don't they arrest anyone who is found without a permit to be in the military zone? I heard people get their head shaved and sometimes tortured before they are sent to a labor camp more brutal than our own. After their sentence is over, they are deported and banned from the Heartland for life. That is what I hear anyway," Bobby said.

"Those worries don't apply to us," James replied.

"Are you sure Dad? We are floating into the most secretive military base on the planet," Bobby said.

"Every military zone has secrets son, and these day what isn't a closed military zone? You talk about being hungry in that work camp, what do you think it will be like when the borders close their doors to the Heartland's bread basket. There will be starvation and desperation for the majority as cost of food inflates through the roof, while Peel's cronies make unprecedented profits," James said.

"That is sort of the way the work camps felt like. Hunger was shared by everyone except the guards," Bobby said.

"A militarized dictatorship's prime responsibility is not to connect to the common people, but to protect the

Heartland with all its might. A mere overpriced wall can never do that. These top priority mobility permits don't expire, ever. No door will be closed for us. We have special permits. We have honorary status in this land of Mina. We will be just as connected as we were in Tut territory during the good old days before the fools voted for President Peel and wore buttons saying anyone but Coaltonstone and immigrating workers to undermine citizen miners. Peel is not only closing borders to unregulated travel between the people, he is closing borders to trade, so he can pander to his Exclusion League cronies' business interests. Peel's cronies are always complaining that they cannot compete with Minese products. I ordered our dinner. Alex, I mean Stan said he might join us but he is guarding the guards who are guarding our precious cargo. Soon the collapsible bridge will open, and we will be welcomed by Ono and by all the movers and shakers of Mina. We will be welcomed with loud cheers and clapping and even though the military zone is closed to most foreigners, it will be open to us because we are here to fund the revolution. We are refusing to be defined by our circumstances or how other people say about us, we are defining ourselves by our deeds. We are the first to make this technology work, this is who we are,, what will define us, not President Peel, not the naysayers who said, 'anyone but Coaltonstone', and we are now the Newmans, still family, still blood, and no one can or will be allowed to destroy that bond between us, never," James said as thumped his fist on the armrest of his chair.

Chapter 2

March 20th 2031, around 3:00 PM

"I have called this meeting for three reasons, and John, put your phone away or I will request, correction, I will order you to put your phone in this basket until I finalize this meeting with a firm tap of my gravel," Mayor Stern ordered.

"Will this meeting be long, I have to meet some of the militia members for coffee?" John Bell asked. As head of security for Mine Five, another Big Seven Coal Group subsidiary, owned and operated by James Coaltonstone, he had few boundaries to follow. John Bell was making extra cash on the side for his surveillance work for the Brotherhood. John took his secret job very seriously.

"This meeting will end when I say it ends? On whose authority, John did your security team, along with Pitville militia storm the Buzzard Creek Tent City last night?" Mayor Stern asked.

"We were receiving noise complaints and Pitville's Chief of police, Florence Cuff, requested my assistance. As head of security I requested the militia's assistance Sir, because the police department and my security team, do not have the manpower to respond safely to an armed uprising. The camp has grown, we estimate that there are about 1,200 plus, people, including women and children living there, but we really don't know, sir. Our moles told us that the riff raff living there had machine guns, and all sorts of weapons, so we responded, with that intelligence in mind, Sir" John Bell replied,"

"You call what happened last night in the Buzzard Creek Tent City has an outcome of intelligence? Is it no wonder that I spend my days feeling that I am being watched even though I can't ever prove it? I have militias shooting unarmed migrants. And if that is not enough, now I am facing the scandal that women and children were shot by stray bullets in their sleep, at the Buzzard Creek Tent City, which the miners are now calling home for their colony. And it is happening right under my nose, without me knowing, until after the fact.

"There are also illegals living in that camp, Sir," John Bell interjected.

"And why are we calling those workers illegals? We used to call them undocumented workers. Those migrants are willing to work in inhuman conditions, even in Mine Five. For decades those workers have laid track, cleared land, handled impurities and were willing to be paid by long tons while citizen miners were only willing to be paid for standard tons," Mayor Stern said.

"The media is calling the event, which happened last night a massacre, Sir, and are demanding access to the site, along with the Red Cross," Susan Jones said.

"No one is getting into Buzzard Creek Tent City. It is under martial law at the present time. We are building a wall around the tent city. No one enters or leaves, without a security clearance, from me or a member of my security team. Buzzard Creek Tent City the site is being treated as a warzone. My orders have been handed down to me from Government's Official Directors, Sir," John Bell said.

"Those people have the right to strike. They have lost their jobs, their homes, and they are families living together at the camp, because they don't want to lose each other," Susan Jones said.

"It is a tragic situation, but we are living in tragic times. It sounds like the uprising in the camp is being contained, if not overkilled," Mayor Stern said.

"It is Sir, not overkilled sir, just contained," John Bell replied.

"On to the next crisis. We have good reason to believe that a portion of our coalface is on fire, which could explain why there is so much smoke that is spreading into our air, from our sidewalk," Mayor Stern said.

"That explains why my asthma is so bad. When are going to fix it?" Susan Jones asked.

"I don't know Susan. Now on to the third issue, we have received an eviction notice from the Minese Authority. The Minese administration is demanding that I hand over all city assets to them or face rage and fire, as if we didn't have enough rage and fire already. Oh, I almost forget, we have a fourth issue. Are you making a note of this, Susan? " Mayor Stern asked.

"I certainly am Sir," Susan Jones replied.

"I have another notice from the Government's Official Directors' office demanding more funds from our treasury, as if we had tons of funds lying idle in our treasury," Mayor Stern complained.

"This is wartime, Sir. Things get rough in wartime. People say and do things they don't do in times of peace. But usually in wartime people feel less direct poverty. They get paychecks to fight," John Bell said.

"I understand why John is glued to his phone. President Peel is tweeting, what he is calling a very presidential announcement, relating to his newest proclamation of another national emergency so he can acquire more money from the defense budget to fund the wall expansion and to install more flags and windmills," Susan Jones, Mayor Stern's secretary explained.

"Windmills?" Mayor Stern asked.

"Yes Sir, lots of windmills," Susan replied. "President Peel is promising that the windmills will remain, until the day Mina agrees to pay for it," Susan said.

"That could be a long time coming," Mayor Stern said.

"I don't know," John Bell replied. "Once the Minese population start coming down with windmill related cancer, they will be demanding to pay for our wall, as long as we take away the windmills," John Bell said.

"Regardless if the Minese people develop windmill related cancers, or not, the Minese people will never pay for a wall that is meant to keep them out," Mayor Stern said.

"President Peel is promising on Twitter that the windmills will stay until the Minese people pay for the wall. President Peel is also promising more exciting rallies, where he will be shouting at, what he calls the Fake News Crew and he will be signing bibles. President Peel is promising more vetoes through Twitter, which he says will make Twitter great and presidential. He also altered the design of our flag so that a younger picture of his face, though faded, can be seen in the background," Susan said.

"Sir, you look peevish, are you okay?" John Bell asked.

"Of course I am not okay. You are letting that stupid twitter thing distract you from the people you are sharing a room with, and you are not listening to a word what I am saying," Mayor Stern shouted.

"I was listening, Sir," Susan Jones said.

"Thank you, Susan. I was talking to John, though. I will repeat what I just said. I have in my hand a notice that the Tut Territory is being accused of stealing Tut Island from Mina. This document insinuates that the sale and related treaties between Tut Territory and the Minese Heartland are void, because at the time the contracts were settled, the Minese had been coerced, which makes, according to them, the historical contractual agreement null and void. In my other hand I have land acquisition orders from President Peel's administration ordering us to declare our citizen's private property as Tut Territory state property. According to this letter all these properties must be make room to build President Peel's wall, which this current national emergency validates. The letter in my left hand decrees that Mina owns Tut Island and the sale that was agreed upon between our two governments during the middle nineteenth century, is deemed as void by the New Heartland Minese Administration. Both letters are written in typical form letter style and were probably spit out by the bureau's robots on both sides of this strange and unexpected conflict. The letter from the Minese Government signed, by someone called Ono. The one from our side is signed by the G.O.D. authority," Mayor Stern explained. "Maybe we would all be better off if the entire west coast became a country on its own and just let those two super powers fight it out without our involvement.

"Sir, you are joking aren't you?" John Bell said.

"I might be. Sometimes I just don't know which side some people are actually on," Mayor Stern replied.

"I am on your side, Sir. And I have no doubt how important Tut Island is to the Tut Territory administration. We should all be very proud to be are part of the great Tut Territory super power. Why would we want to give up our power by becoming a speck of an island that no one has ever heard of, administered by the Minese government which is technically at war with our own government? I have no problem knowing what side I am on, Sir, Do you?" John Bell asked.

"Of course I love my country, if you are implying that I don't, you are dead wrong," Mayor Stern said.

"Dead is an interesting word, Sir" John Bell said.

"John, please develop some empathy for the people you are working with. I can think of a few reasons why it would be easier to give up than to fight the Minese. Our Pitville economy is no longer sustainable. The Pitville Fire Department is over its yearly budget again, and it is only March, and Mina owns trillions of dollars of the debt that we owe," Mayor Stern said.

"As Head of Security, I would blame those fires on all those homeless people loitering in the park and all over town," John Bell said.

"Why would homeless people burn down one of their own camps, and the bridge that was sheltering that camp? Why would homeless people burn down a second hand store which funds some of programs designed to re-integrate families which are being impacted by the closing of the mines?" Susan Jones asked.

"Why would homeless people start an uprising in Buzzard Creek Tent City, or any other homeless people camp? People act irrationally, when they are ignorant and have had one too many," John Bell interjected.

"Why are we are calling striking miners homeless people?" Susan asked.

"We call them homeless, because they are homeless?" John Bell shouted as he banged his coffee mug on Mayor Stern's desk.

"John, please," Mayor Stern said.

"Those people are homeless because their homes were taken to Coalton Two, and the mines have closed in Pitville," Susan Jones said.

"That is right, they have no homes, no jobs and are creating chaos and mayhem in Pitville as if they owned this town," John Bell replies.

"Did you see that pile of business licenses that aren't being picked up on Edna's desk as you walked by, John? Our merchants are leaving Pitville. And on Melanie's desk, there is a lawsuit filed by a group of homeless tenants..." Mayor Stern began to say before John interrupted him.

"How can tenants be homeless?" John asked the Mayor as Susan rolled her eyes.

"They are suing us because of last month's water main breaking, which led to their eviction. To add insult to their injury, security refused to allow them into Pitville City Hall to attend our council meeting, because they were homeless people," Mayor Stern said.

"The group of homeless people I did not allow in city hall are homeless people, so technically they don't have a residence so they don't actually live in Pitville. The mines are closed so the miners I recognized technically don't work in Pitville anymore, so what business do they have loitering in our city hall?" John said.

"I have problems piling up on desks all over this city hall and we have no money to solve not even one of them. But we seem to have plenty of money to send to Government's Official Directors in Tut Metropolis. The question isn't whether I will win another election, the question is whether I want to win another election," Mayor Stern replied.

"Sir, don't take it all so hard, we are in a position of strength. The eviction notice from the Minese administration sent us, is either a joke or just another act of war, and we need to secure our parameters the best way we can, until we are issued new orders from G.O.D. Imagine if the Alaska was issued a similar notice? It would be seen as a joke," John Bell interjected.

"I am the Mayor of Pitville, and if my town is being declared a colony by a foreign power, a country that we are at war with. I must have a line of defence to protect our assets and to protect my people," Mayor Stern said.

"What people? Once Mine Five closed, or at least closed to human miners, and all the so called workers' houses were moved to Coalton Two, the remaining people were either left to die or to fend for themselves as our local economy collapsed," Susan said.

"Susan, shut up," John Bell said.

"Silence hides everything. We were told automation would free workers from the drudgery of work, but like usually we were lied to. We were told that the owners of these robots and automated systems were going to be charged some form of income tax, but the whole process has been tied up by President Peel and the Exclusion League in court, even before President Peel was elected. People who don't have jobs are being starved to death and sometimes burned alive by death squad militias," Susan said.

"Susan please, you are depressing me," Mayor Stern said.

"Someone must have sent President Peel the same document," John Bell said.

"Doesn't President Peel do anything else besides tweet?" Susan asked. "It is like the entire world is turning against us and all he is doing is going on about how his wall will stop invaders and nothing else will," Susan commented while she stared at John Bell who was staring back at her.

"Fool. That wall could be jumped over by any drone or flying object. Being so walled in can only make us feel more claustrophobic than we are already being made to feel. As the space allocated to public use shrinks as walls of barbwire surround us, we are going to feel very over-crowded and people will start turning against each other. How do we get in and out of Pitville quickly during a real emergency?" Mayor Stern asked.

"That is classified Sir, only people in authority know how, Sir, but trust me, there is a plan," John Bell said as Mayor Stern stared at him in disbelief.

"Then who am I, a munchkin from Oz? Mayor Stern asked.

"No sir, you are the mayor of Pitville," John Bell replied.

"That is right. I am an elected official, which gives me authority to question the sanity and appropriateness of this project which will cost us billions and could be even breached," Mayor Stern said.

"Sir with all respect, your jurisdiction rests in the municipality. You are not part of the G.O.D. team," John Bell said.

"The world is run and managed by bots and is under surveillance by flying drones, and President Peel's big solution to the Minese threat of turning Tut Island into one of their colonies, is a wall? What century does President Peel think we are living in?"

"I actually voted for President Peel, Sir," John Bell

confessed.

"I am not surprised that you voted for him, John. He doesn't seem to ever go outside unless there is a photo opportunity waiting for him. He wears suits that must cost him thousands of dollars, which never fit him right and then he accessorizes with those super long ties that he sometimes uses duct tape to keep in place. Why does he bother?

"You women don't understand anything. Yes, he wears those expensive suits not just to flaunt his wealth but to flaunt his independence, his suits may look like they are wearing him, but he is still in control because he dresses for himself. While you women spend half the day dressing up to upstage each other, men of means often do the opposite. We men save our time by dressing down, while instituting a timeless bond by not upstaging each other, which of course promotes the message that I just dress for myself as we all should, while women dress for success by upstaging each other," John said.

"You, single men don't get it. It is our wives that dress us, or at least let us out of the house only after we pass inspection," Mayor Stern said.

"Is that the way it is with you and Mrs. Stern?" John asked.

"Does it even matter, Sir? We don't have much of a town left to get dressed up or down for. We are living in a shell of a town that has little economic activity and doesn't seem to be huge priority for the Government's Official Directors. Their criteria, protocols and declarations of what is and what is not, are pretty much self-serving, as far as I can see," Susan said.

"Susan, shut up," John ordered.

"Susan please just take notes and when this meeting is adjourned please leave them next to the shredder," Mayor Stern said. "I have no idea where James Coaltonstone is, he has basically disappeared into the abyss."

"Hold on my phone is ringing," Mayor Stern said as he answered his phone. "What do you mean your car disappeared in a sinkhole? Did you phone a tow truck?

"Ted, please listen to me, there was a water main break on Sixth Avenue. I was grocery shopping and parked our car in the wrong place at the wrong time, and when I went to get our car it was disappearing in the hole," Martha Stern said

"Are you okay, give me a sec, Martha, I am going to adjourn this meeting? We can't just pack up and leave town, I have duties and obligations, and we don't have a car now. I know there are shortages in the stores. There isn't a law against that," Ted said as he looked around the room. "Meeting is adjourned, I have to go and rent a car and pick up Mrs. Stern. I remember when Pitville was one of the most beautiful towns on the Island, I wish we could back to those days."

"Isn't that the whole dilemma of Paradise Lost, Sir?" Susan replied.

"Susan, shut up," John and Mayor Stern said in unison.

"People complain about the declining of quality of life in Pitville. People blame the homeless people. The homeless people are victims too. They are being displaced so that the landlords can charge higher rents, and many of those landlords are members of the Exclusion League, which are backing of President Peel. Human workers are being replaced with bots. Quality of a person and a society comes from within the heart. Following heartless role models that are dictating the reality that in the end we must all live with. We need to be concerned for all stakeholders, not just for the privileged few," Susan replied.

"Shut up Susan," John replied. "You are the last one who should be lecturing us about reality."

Chapter 3

March 20th 2031, around 4:00 PM

"How are we supposed to report on the massacre that happened last night, when they are building a wall around the site, and are not allowing anyone in?" Dianne asked. "The rumors are that women and children were shot by stray bullets, but we can't get any information, or anything. We were told by John Bell, that if we send a drone over the wall, they will shoot it down, and declare us, as members of Fake News, enemy of the people."

"When President Peel and his Exclusion League backers do their 'managing by ego' routine, the entire Tut population is either terrorized or ignored. And to survive in such an environment people harden themselves while wanting to avenge the loss of their loved ones and who they used to be when they were still living in a free country. Tutonians have been hardened by extreme economic policy and food insecurity, and whatever goes on Pitville seems to stay in Pitville. President Peel isn't just going to bring instability and ruin to the Tut territory, he is ruining our loyal trading partners across the globe, and now this massacre. Who is going to want to trade with us, when new gets out that women and children were killed why they slept? President Peel is going to make it impossible for us to live our dreams when we are being forced to live his dream. It is like being in a nightmare that you never wake up from," Jackson said.

"At least, now we can wake up and face the world together, Jackson," Dianne said.

"Yeah, despite it all, living as a family makes me incredibly happy. Having family changes everything. Whatever hardship people must bare being with family makes hardships tolerable. That is probably why families fought to stay together and called themselves a miner colony, while camping in the Buzzard Creek Tent City," Jackson replied.

"What does anyone know about the massacre? Does anyone know who was massacred? How do we report a massacre if we can't get into the site?" Dianne asked. "They are not even allowing the Red Cross in."

"The times today are much worse than when we were young, Di. When I was young, I vowed to myself to honor my dreams, and to make those dreams my destiny, so that I could have something to believe in, even during times when I am forced to take a path of someone else's choosing. I always hoped that I could contribute to a better world. Tut Territory has grown so big, people lose perspective of what really matters in life. And what matters in life, is being alive. I want to raise David and Mary to have the privileges that make being Buynese so wonderful but to cherish their connection to the Minese people," Jackson said.

"I want that too for our kids. I want our kids to understand that the classification of the Buynese and Minese as two different and separate races has no scientific basis. This new racial profiling is made up to. We are living in terrible times when the creators of a biased and horrific social order, can create so much mistrust that they are able to convince the general public that they need a wall to keep foreigners out when the wall might be getting built to keep us in, or to even hide a massacre," Dianne said.

"Well that is what life is all about these days. It is one massive rat race to the finish line. We live on a planet where wild animals would eat us if they had half a chance. Our extreme weather destroys so much of what we build to protect ourselves from the weather. Life is a vicious circle. For many people life will get much harder than they could ever imagine, and the public relations people will tell them how they feel their pain, and they will get 10 cents on the dollar in compensation, or no compensation at all. They build homes so they can relax and enjoy the comfort of family and friends while watching nature from their windows. One day, they will be told that they are living on a flood plain, not by the real estate people who sold them the properties, and added tens of thousands of dollars for an unblocked view, no they will be told by first responders. And then after President Peel and his Exclusion League expropriate the land, they will put up more border walls. Sooner than later, we will all be walled in, and so will nature. After the land on our side of the wall is turned into a park, President Peel can charge people to fees for fishing permits, and fees for walking in nature permits. And as the waters rise up and the lightning sets forests on fire, this planet is still our home. Our bodies were made to live on this planet, and there is no other planet, that we know of, that we actually belong. And belonging is why family matters so much. Without family, home and friends, we would just harden, all alone, before nature kills us. It is just a matter of when. And once you reach a crossroad, you never know where you will land up unless you have a map to plan your destination, and a compass to direct you while walking through fog and confusion. Often you just land up running around in circles if you are not careful, you could waste your entire life feeling lost," Jackson replied.

"Jackson, really. You sound so gloomy. Life is what you make it. We have always found ways to move forward and we will find ways to help Mary and David move forward, together. Time heals," Dianne said.

"Sure time heals, if it doesn't kill you first," Jackson said.

"Come on Jackson, you are depressing me. We report the bad things that happen to other people, but then we walk away, we go home, and detach ourselves from what we have just seen. And that is how we stay sane. We detach and let time heal us and have a glass of wine," Dianne said.

"Maybe we have just been lucky so far. A lot of people race against time, and before they know it, their life is over," Jackson said.

"Maybe that is true, but the next stage of our lives, our family life, has just begun," Dianne said.

"The Coaltonstones move forward at a faster pace, than anyone else I have ever met. They make their own decisions and they choose to ignore the limits that are imposed on them by others, especially by the bureaucrats who advance by classifying people and pushing them through the system," Jackson asked.

"And now they are massacring them. I always though this new trend of shouting insults at us and calling us fake news is being used to make noise, so they can cover something very big, up," Dianne said.

"We devoted our lives to report and broadcast events and conflicts that are happening all over the world. We had to travel to those places and sleep in lumpy beds. It would have been much easier if we just faked all the stories that we reported, wouldn't it have been, Dianne?" Jackson said.

"It is bad enough that people are being made to feel irrelevant. But if they are being massacred, we are entering an era that reminds me of the past. People are losing their jobs and their homes and their ties to the world around them. That is what the Peel administration exploits, as far as I can see. He exploits the nothingness people are feeling, deep inside. And that nothingness can lead to accepting nihilism, especially when everything that they had hoped for, can never happen. Waiting for a dream that they will never be allowed to live is just living a life of futility. There will be a lot to this war that will surprise us. A lot that we won't be able to see. If rumors are true that the Minese are building a military base on the dark side of the moon while President Peel's plan for national defense is to build a wall, sounds like a bad joke. No wonder people believe that resistance is futile. Rigid authority, hidden behind fake gods and easy answers, fool us into believing the lie, that we are not one world. Only a fool would be depleting defense reserve funds to build a wall while imposing tariffs on products of long-term allies, will only alienate us from allies, possibly when we need them the most," Dianne said.

"You are right, of course. No one wants to fail, and many will kill to succeed," Jackson said.

"Or kill to avenge for their failure," Dianne interjected.

"Easier to blame the messenger. Especially when they become overwhelmed at all the unfair limits and obstacles there really are, blocking their path. And for some people, there is nothing for them. And almost everyone knows that. Everyone needs some sort of social mobility, some food security and a bit of opportunity so that they are able to improve the quality of their lives," Jackson said.

"Do you really think President Peel and his Exclusion League backers care about our quality of life or those his cronies may have massacred last night, in the Buzzard Creek Tent City? President Peel calls the press fake news over and over again. He must really fear ability of the press to open a window so that ordinary people are able to see what is going on in unknown places. I also think President Peel fears young people who want to know the truth. Young people need to know the truth because they have to plan a life for themselves, so they can be where they want to be, ten years from now," Dianne said.

"Everyone has to guess what might happen to them in ten years' time," Jennifer said.

"I am not talking about guessing, Jennifer, I am talking about planning and negotiating your turns in life. I am talking about which profession to choose, who you choose to share your life and time with," Jackson said.

"Don't forget forces beyond my control created a huge hole in my life, when they shot down Mathew. I know most people want to feel like they are growing not decaying, and I feel the same way. But plans. My plans have been shot down the day Mathew was shot down. I am a different person without Mathew. I have a huge hole in my life, now. All my plans for the future have been shattered. We protected each other and I never felt alone, because I knew I had a loyal partner in Mathew. I know aging at my age is about growing and I know I have to prepare myself for when I get to be your age, and when it is all downhill from there," Jennifer said.

"Speak for yourself," Jackson said.

"I just mean after a certain point in time it is all about going downhill and decaying, but I never expected to lose Mathew so soon. And now I have this huge hole in my life," Jennifer said.

"I have felt that hole in my life many times, and I fight to not get lost in it. I always feel that way after people I loved disappeared, died or were killed by who knows who. People usually experience the loss you are feeling when they are much older. Jennifer, promise me, that you won't get trapped in that hole. Once you are trapped in that hole, you may never get out and your loss could freeze you in time. You have to continue moving and growing with your life before time runs out and it becomes much harder to change the direction that your life is taking," Jackson said.

"I know what you are saying, but I wonder a lot about hate and war, especially when I feel surrounded by all this rage, hate and desperation that is feeding this war. So when old people are experiencing that horrible hole in their lives, they must be feeling themselves decaying too. So in a way, they are losing themselves. So they see us and must feel envious knowing that time is on our side because we are young, while time is running out for them. So they send us to fight the wars between mad men who are leading us into a global madness. Are old people so envious of us, they hate us and want us dead? When we wake up and we aren't feeling like we are decaying and rotting and dying like old people, they must wish that they were young again, so they make us miserable by giving us no free time while forcing us to fight their wars. Why send us off to war just to be killed? And if we don't get killed, we return to a place we no longer belong," Jennifer interjected.

"I can't believe that Tut Territory is willing be turned into a civil warzone?" Dianne said.

"I can," Jackson replied.

"I have seen news clip of you two leaping over barriers and fearlessly reporting from warzones as bullets were being shot around you and explosions were raging as background noise," Jennifer said.

"Wouldn't that be awful if Pitville became just another warzone?" Dianne asked.

"Once there is that much violence the ruling authorities get to declare state of emergency and become more authoritarian," Jackson said.

"I know. And banning the press is one of those things that they do," Dianne said.

"I bet when you were young, you just knew you wanted to see the truth for yourself. That is exactly the way Mathew and I used to feel about writing and taking photographs. We knew were living during a turning point in history, and we never wanted to forget what could have been, especially when we have aged out of our idealism. We wanted to share what our eyes are able to see beyond this strange war of global warming, that pits everyone against each other, for food, water, land and air. Yet the forces that are supposed to be in control are so out of reach and invisible it is hard to believe that they really exist," Jennifer said.

"We still want to see things for ourselves and to show others, isn't that right, Jackson?" Dianne asked.

"Sort of. When I was growing up, the threat of nuclear war was always in our face, and scared the hell out of me. Being burned to death in my sleep seemed like a fate worse than death, and the fear of it, haunted me. Made me more nihilistic and fatalistic. I only became idealistic after I started to work with Dianne," Jennifer said.

"I can't imagine you ever being nihilistic, Mr. Green," Jennifer said.

"I wouldn't ever have called Jackson nihilistic. He always seems to believe in something and the value for what surrounds us. A real nihilist, is like Peel

"Please, Jennifer, you are making me feel old, please call me Jackson," Jackson interjected.

"But you are old, Mr. Green," Jennifer protested.

"No, President Peel is old, and I think at times he defines what is nihilistic and fatalistic. President Peel is a big time influencer. President Peel and the Exclusion League are control freaks. They hate everyone and everything that they cannot control," Dianne explained.

"Was Jackson really nihilistic when he was young?" Jennifer asked.

"I don't believe Jackson was ever nihilistic though I think he has a tendency to feel fatalistic when he is exposed to too much bad news at once. Isn't that right Jackson"?

"I suppose so. I also get very claustrophobic when I feel there is no way out of a bad situation, especially when I was younger," Jackson replied.

"Can you really remember that far back?" Jennifer asked.

"Of course I can. It feels like yesterday." Jackson said.

"What was it like when you two first met?" Jennifer wanted to know.

"When I first met Di I felt shivers take over my body, and I had to leave the room," Jackson said.

"I remember you leaving the room and I had no idea why," Dianne said.

"And now you know," Jackson said.

"I remember how he would stand there, in a warzone, holding the camera, without even a twitch, as bullets were being shot and explosions were being set off right in front of us," Dianne said.

"I think when we first met, we both realized that we had similar values and that we felt an urgency for evidence based journalism, which could protect what we valued from the corruption of the most powerful. We wanted to give a voice to the things both of us valued and could see were being threatened in silence," Jackson said.

"Trying to bring world peace and end world hunger were umbrella goals. It is the little things that accumulate into huge global problems when not solved and just ignored. We wanted to inspire and move people all over the world so that they would question the mindless destruction war causes and then to find a way to end it," Dianne said. "And I appreciated how handsome Jackson was too."

"Were you disappointed when you realized how impossible it would be to end war and world hunger, I know I am. There is so much being wasted," Jennifer asked.

"Sometimes I do, but I do believe it is possible and those goals are not unreasonable especially when world war is contributing to global warming and threatening human societies and survival. At times I feel overwhelmed when I think how nuclear war and global warming could perpetuate each other," Jackson said.

"And such carnage would be a Nihilist's dream not Jackson's" Dianne said.

"President Peel seems to be using nihilism as a weaponized form of psychology, which traps people into a pessimistic frame of mind. And this hopelessness is dividing people," Jackson said.

"We still believe in our ideals and Jackson has been by my side since our early twenties," Dianne asked.

"Thank God for you, Di," Jackson said. "The day I met Di, and started to work by her side, it was like a dark cloud that had surrounded me was lifted and I could see the future again.

Global warming is a hassle that is for sure but under President Peel, it seems like the nuclear threat is returning and add that to global warming, we might go extinct like the Neanderthals," Jackson said.

"In some ways it is better for us, personally, now. We have a lot of experience and we have a seen how the human condition in some places have improved beyond our wildest dreams, but in other places the human condition seems hopeless," Dianne said.

"Of course it is. I am sure there were people who would love to shout insults at us that everything is fake. But without media, there would be no window for outsiders to look into. Those people who act as if they hate us, would be shut out from the inner goings on of their own country, and they would grow to be even more alienated and sad as individuals. Peel might go to great lengths to legitimize their hate, but that doesn't mean he would be willing to include them in the decision making process. A dictator is a dictator no matter how many rallies and concerts he holds for his supporters. They go to these rallies, and are able to lord over others while moving around in a mob. Most power they probably ever had in their lives," Jackson said.

"It could have been hopeless for Mary and David too, if you weren't there willing and able to share your lives with them. David could still be under all that rubble in Coalton Two and who knows where Mary would be by now. Probably sitting in a holding cell waiting for an opening that may never happen, as she ages out of the system," Jennifer said.

"A lot of people are waiting for openings that never happen. Some people are going to want to avenge themselves for their lack of access to the inside workings and job opportunities, while bots replace our jobs, one by one," Jackson said.

"No bot could replace you and Di," Jennifer interjected.

"I think these days when front door access is not open to ordinary people, you have to find the backdoor. The paths to power and wealth seem to have always been rigged by barriers and always seemed to have favored the privileged," Dianne said.

"Privilege and prejudice is a two sided coin, as far as I can see" Jennifer said.

"We were very lucky to have been given openings and to have found job opportunity and to experience life in so many different places without feeling like an outsider. We have had a life time to develop who we are, and I have always found fulfillment as an independent personality," Dianne said.

"I always wonder if President Peel gets any kind of fulfillment from what he does every day. He bet that anger he is always sharing on twitter is probably not just that he is his biggest supporter of his wall and most people know that wall is nothing but an inside joke, even amongst the Exclusion League Elite. He is probably incredibly angry that he cannot control how the force of time is changing him. It must feel that time is no longer on his side. While people my age are still growing, he is decaying. That must really freak him out. Time is on our side because we are young. And time will sooner than later run out on President Peel because he is so old," Jennifer said.

"And what scares me is that we could get someone worse than President Peel. We could get someone who rushes to judgment even faster than President Peel, for the sake of profit instead of for mere self-gratification," Jackson said.

"You mean a robot?" Jennifer asked.

"No I don't meant a robot, though that would not be a bad idea. I am kidding. I don't know. They remember the lines to play the game, but they never say who they are or what they are actually feeling, because if they do, they risk being carried away in a straitjacket, at their own expense. If they would only design a system to humanize the process of living," Jackson said.

"Or at least they could correct their computer generated errors before they scare people to death," Dianne replied.

"That is how demagogues take advantage of the weakness within our bureaucracy and our population. To win against Peel, we must finance a revolution from both sides of the border. If Peel can't dictate terms of trade to others he closes in on them and puts up walls which isolate and stunt development. Closing the borders to engineer social divisions in development is nothing new. When the gap between the haves and the have nots polarizes people, they start demanding for revolution and change not just in leadership but how things are done. The Exclusion League insiders grow more dependent on the demagogue bureaucracy when trade between countries comes to a standstill. I am still not sure if the wall is meant to keep the outsiders out, or the insiders in. Once people start demanding for a revolution, Peel will probably declare a crisis, and close borders in the name of national security. Once cost of living becomes unaffordable for the majority, they will demand a revolution, a movement, a turning of the tide. People are educated to be separated from nature and each other. How can people know how to be objective or integrate with different kinds of people if they never get the chance? As long as people are brought up in segregated cultures, they will be socially engineered to fight each other to the death. All they will need is guns," Jackson said

"Socially engineered egos and hurt feelings respond like pawns to President Peel's magnetic personality. Perfect conditions for the master of the masses to manipulate as he promotes himself as a man of the people. Perfect conditions for a demagogue to manipulate. President Peel uses fear, pride and ignorance to draw people to him and his cause, like a magnet in a polarized world" Dianne replied.

"Pulling people towards his magnetic personality and pushing the people into giving up their power," Jackson said.

"We must inspire a questioning of the process so people don't give up their power, because when they give up their power, they are also giving up their democratic rights and freedoms. The revolution begins from within. To question the lie is the first step. Our job as journalists is more important than ever before," Dianne said.

"That is what I want to do too. Not just question the lie, but to give truth visibility," Jennifer said.

"When a cult is built on prejudice and ignorance the last thing people like that are going to want is knowledge and critical thinking. Peel and his Exclusion League need to turn people into faddists and alarmists so that they willingly give up their power without a struggle," Jackson said.

"We are all prone to bias. And many people deny their margin of error. No one is one hundred percent right. Even people who share their stories with us are often prone to telling only their side of the story. It is not really reasonable to expect more from ordinary people, and President Peel exploits that tendency in people to see things from their center of the universe," Dianne said.

"And President Peel's droning voice I think adds to his ability to entrance people into giving up their power," Jennifer said. "

"His voice either puts people to sleep or mesmerizes them so they never take the time to filter out the lies," Dianne said.

"The people expect us to filter out the lies, but it is near impossible to do that when President Peel is promising the impossible," Jackson interjected.

"Proving the impossible is the same as trying to prove a negative. Assuming innocence and staying concerned with the positive elevates us into a higher realm of reality that just feels better and is easier to understand. Why use force when exiling people weakens them naturally?" Dianne said.

"It seems to me the Exclusion League doesn't just exclude people who oppose them, they omit facts, so that promising something that is impossible seems to be possible," Jennifer said.

"We are damned if we do and damned if we don't. Proving a negative is almost as impossible as President Peel's promises. We call him on it, we are called fake news, while his Exclusion League backers targets anyone who opposes them and condemns them to a life of exclusion. President Peel's self-serving omissions of other people's reality is probably what helped him win the election. He depends on people assuming he meant something that he omitted when most likely the frustration of facing his omission can take over people's minds and make them look very ill," Dianne said.

"As in psychological warfare that doesn't shed blood or break bones," Jackson said.

"I still have power over my mind, the identity crushers haven't got to me yet," Jennifer said.

"That is a positive thought," Jackson said.

"I am not so crushed I don't care about my future, the problem is I don't know, this new administration doesn't seem to be planning for the long-term future. Why would they care what is left behind for ordinary people my age? They hold on to their authority over us without concern that the bubble they have produced is going to burst. If they don't care about the crash why should I even expect them to care about where Mathew is? To them, he is just collateral damage. We don't even vote, not yet anyway. I wonder if I will actually live long enough to vote. Wonder if Mathew wishes we had succeeded in lowering the voting age. Would it have made a difference? Probably not, except we would feel that our voices counted for something. The way the civic system works now, we made to be and feel voiceless," Jennifer said.

Chapter 4

"They never let us get to the next level, do they?" Jennifer said.

"I know that it feels that way, Jennifer," Maria said, "but if you are patient, things usually will work out."

"For who? I feel like my growth has been stunted, and my life has been put on hold, and all I want to know is how to get my life moving forward again," Jennifer said. "Dianne, how did you get started?"

"I just walked in, auditioned, and then I was hired," Dianne explained.

"Yes, but Dianne always makes it sound so easy, actually there were hundreds of people being auditioned, and they chose her," Jackson added.

"What did you do that gave you the edge over the other candidates, Dianne?" Jennifer asked.

"I really don't know," Dianne said. "I guess it was just luck."

"No Di, it wasn't just luck. Dianne followed her dreams, in the same way that I was following my dreams," Jackson interjected. "We intentionally made our own dreams our destiny, and we were able to create the life that we wanted to live. Our dreams anchored us so we wouldn't become victims of a fate. It also helped that Dianne had the look. Dianne had the star quality that you either have or don't have."

"Sooner or later star power fades. I want to grow my creative power that Mathew was growing. He saw the beauty in the nature around him but he was also painfully aware of human suffering as being part of the human condition, and photographed it moment by moment," Jennifer said.

"Did Mathew create any enemies? Anyone who hated him because he was taking pictures or did you hear anyone accusing him of being crazy or a deviant? Did you hear any aggressive catcalls from people saying they saw him taking photographs while flyking? Anything like that?" Jackson asked.

"Who doesn't get talked to like that if you look under 25?"

"Today I was at one of those big chain restaurants, and I had this song that kept playing in my head, so I sat down, and wrote it out, before I ordered. The person sweeping the floor came over to me, and started to scold me in an angry tone and told me that I better buy something, or she would phone the police on me. She said that I couldn't just sit there and write, and since I knew better to argue with her, I said I understood and I finished writing the song, anyway. Then she said that "I better not be dealing drugs" as if everyone my age was dealing drugs," Jennifer said

"Where ever you go people are thinking they are fighting the war on drugs by attacking kids, especially kids who are alone and have more things than they have. The noble President Peel with his face plastered all over his brand of wine, Champaign, beer and perfumes. His followers respond to President Peel's fifteen minutes of hate by power debranding the opposition. It is not just about the insults and stigmatization, it is about dismissing and projecting negativity onto others, as a distraction from the taking away of democratic power. It is frightening to be targeted and talked to like that by the Exclusion League's state sponsored violence is really demoralizing. As if we need any more exclusion to cover up for lack of solutions and impossible promises that could never have been met," Jackson said.

"Can you sing it?" Dianne asked.

"Sing what?" Jennifer asked.

"Your song," Dianne replied.

"Yeah, I can sing it when I play my etherplayer. I have never sang it before with others listening though," Jennifer explained.

"We are all being watched and listed to, we just don't see it," Jackson interjected.

"You sound like such a creative person, and my advice for what it is worth, is you have to ignore these people who power trip whenever they get a chance, just because they have a little bit of power to make someone feel beneath them. Always remember who you are. You only live once, and that toxic culture is a drug in itself. Life is too short to waste it on all the grief these people in prejudgment mode, you can get caught up in it, and then they can cause tons of problems for people who are trying to rise above tough circumstances, like you are trying to do," Jackson said.

"It almost like when anyone is kind anymore it is a show of weakness," Jennifer said.

"You can't let those bigots get to you, you need to stay elevated and be an example for a better way," Jackson said.

"That is right, if Jackson took everything to heart, his hair would be a lot shorter today," Dianne said.

"Mathew is very lucky to have you on his side," Jackson said.

"Thank, you Ms. Black, or should I call you Mrs. Green?" Jennifer asked.

"No, I mean just call me Dianne and call Jackson by his first name." Dianne said.

"Why not call Me Mr. Black, I mean Di is our public face. Everyone recognizes Di's face. Me, I am just the guy behind the camera. I might as well be lost in the void of nothingness," Jackson said.

"Di, I am serious. Why can't I take your name? It makes sense that I change my name to your name," Jackson said.

"You guys kill me," Jennifer said.

"I am not making a joke. I think we should be called the Blacks. I want to take your name, Di," Jackson said.

"And please just call me Jackson."

"Can you play your song? Dianne asked.

"Just close your eyes and pretend we are not here," Jackson said.

I

Why did Fate shoot my love down?
Why was my love under attack?
Mathew, all I want is for you to come home to me.
I feel such loss, common when the enemy becomes the boss.

Just another force without a heart, ripping us apart.

II

Mathew, you told me that hate would never win,
As long as our love was able to grow from within.
But look at us now
I hurt so bad, cause I don't know where you are.

III

Mathew, I want you to know
Since you have been gone, I wish I had never let you go.
And if I could have a second chance
I know I would hold on to you tighter,

IV

Because I feel so lost without you,
After fate broke and divided our unity in two.
Dark forces are all around us, created just to surround us.
Then I could hear destiny so near begging me to ignore my fear.

V

I dream that you are with me, my love
Before I awake into this world so tough,
I open my eyes, I see through their disguise,
As my heart starts to break, my hope starts to shake.

VI

While the machines of war,
Grow teeth like a rodent-carnivore.
I need your love more than ever before
To balance what fate has in store.

Chapter 5

March 20th 2031 around 5:00 PM

"Welcome viewers to another news breaking story from Pitville, situated on the East Coast of beautiful Tut Island. I am Dianne Black, with the PPZ bringing to you another live update. Viewers, you must bare with us, we are not being allowed to cover or even enter the Buzzard Creek Tent City, where women and children have been reported to have been massacred while they slept. The Buzzard Creek Tent City, which is housing the displaced miner colony, is under lock down, while a wall is being built around the tent city and will eventually surround them.

We have another story to report, but we are not sure what the story really is, because no one is willing to talk to us from the Big Seven Group and CEO, James Coaltonstone is nowhere to be found. Viewers just look at all those bots, what do you think the story is? Those bots are so shiny and new, as they move into the shaft entrance and out of sight. I suppose they will soon be covered in coal dust. So what do you think viewers? Do you think these bots have been sent to the mine to replace the human workers who used to work the coal face, deep below Pitville? The early Sunday morning explosion, which occurred December 22nd, of last year, triggered several other explosions, which devastated Pitville's mining and resource economy? The Pitville Mine Disaster of 2030 some say, not only closed down the mine but also closed down most of the town. I am Dianne Black, with the PPZ, bringing to you another live update from Pitville brought to you by the municipality of Sunrise Beach, where friends meet and sometimes stay. Back to you Steve."

"Well, that was depressing, wasn't it Jackson? Imagine a world where humans are no longer needed?" Dianne said.

"I was thinking the same thing when I was zooming in and out of the shaft entrance. Something or someone must be watching those bots inside the mine. So is the mine open or closed? Hold on Di, I am getting a phone call from James Coaltonstone.

"Where is he and what does he want?" Dianne asked.

"I don't know. I will put him on the speaker phone," Jackson said.

"This report that I just watching on TV is nothing but fake news. Those bots are going into mine five to do dangerous and dirty work. Work that free men would not do if I paid them. What gives you the right to make up stories up about my enterprise just because I happen to be visiting another continent?" James shouted through the phone.

"Because the story is relevant, and we break stories, that is our job," Jackson shouted back.

"Can you hear me James?" Dianne asked.

"Yes, I heard your little opinion piece and that is all it is. It is fake news not real news," James said.

"We don't broadcast stories to polarize people the way President Peel seems to be doing. The miners want and need jobs, and want and need their homes back," Dianne said.

"Those miners that you put out of work, just wanted to live the way they have always lived, and their fathers before them. They were good, decent people and minded their own business. They didn't spy on people or try to get into their minds, and then devastate them psychologically.

"I sell coal, Peel sells fear and the Exclusion League and its mercenary cyber soldiers swarm across the cybersphere, spreading gossip, hate and all kinds of hurtful misrepresentations," James said.

"At least we found something we agree on," Dianne said.

"Talk about misrepresentation. Human jobs are being replaced all the time. So it matters that you bring in hundreds of bots to do work, which humans used to do. We are always being told that all this automation will free humans to live a life of leisure but all I see are streets full of homeless people who are treated like bums. Banks have been profiting from automation for over fifty years, replacing tellers, and posting huge profits. And that was only the beginning. Sure politicians told us that we were entering an era of leisure, never mentioning that our humanity is being degraded while people are being left to die, homeless and destitute while being stigmatized as alcoholics and junkies. This misrepresentation of reality, what I observe every day, began way before I was even born. News is never free. What we give up is the right to know the truth, but the arguments start because everyone sees everything differently and their own false pride often leading to the prejudicial treatment of others, based on simple things, beyond our control. And you know why so much money is spent on brainwashing the masses, because it works. Convincing people that it is in their best interest to kill each other, for reasons they don't even understand, while human workers are being replaced by as many bots as possible. And it matters," Jackson said.

"Maybe partly what you are saying is true, Jackson, but the other part is just fake news," James replied.

"I know what you are saying James, but these conspiracy theories fuel hate towards journalists, and..." Dianne said.

"Dianne, our vulnerability as human beings is what we have in common. Fate brings us together as human beings because we all suffer as human beings," James said.

"As far as I can see, you suffer a lot less than your workers," Jackson said.

"I provide my workers with food security and I do suffer in my own way. We all have a 'best before' expiry date, and I obviously I have passed mine a few years ago. Bots only need parts and orders to be inputted into their systems. Bots work without needing food or sleep. Bots don't need life-work balance and they obviously don't need to be loved. Bots are expendable and replaceable," James said.

"And you are saying humans aren't?" Dianne asked.

"As long as there are materials to manufacture and re-manufacture bots, in all their different forms, humans are not needed the way they used to be, and that scares me," Jackson said.

"The Exclusion League seems to be spreading a culture that legitimizes the vilifying of human beings and human nature," Dianne said.

"I find the possibility that the Exclusion League could be hiding a secret agenda which intends to escalate present day conflicts into another world war, where millions are exterminated, a very real and frightening threat," Jackson said.

Chapter 6

March 20th 2031 around 6:00 PM

"President Peel is at an all-time high in poles, even though there has been a massacre at the Buzzard Creek Tent City," Jennifer said.

"Alleged massacre," Jackson corrected Jennifer. "The administration is denying that there ever was a massacre, and they are not letting us in, to find evidence," Jackson explained.

"I believe there was one, and I think the poles are fake. The kids that were killed in their bed, and the kids like me, are never included in the poles. We, who haven't been killed or caged yet, have opinions of our own. Those opinions reflect our human condition," Jennifer said.

"You mean inhuman condition. What is going on today is a lot worse than it was when I was your age, and that is really saying something," Jackson said.

"I guess he is allowing some of us to live because we are the ones who will be paying back the debt long after President Peel and his Exclusion League have passed away. There is never money for schools or health care. Our roads and bridges are crumbling but there is no money for infrastructure projects, except the border wall building project," Jennifer said.

"And the wall that they are building around Buzzard Creek Tent City. It must feel like the ones in power are making a pact with the devil, and willing to trade your future so they can get huge tax breaks now," Jackson said.

"No kidding. I could sure use a revolution right now," Jennifer said.

"I think that is exactly what President Peel wants; an uprising that he can crush, if he hasn't done so already. He might say that he is really high in the polls, but compared to other past presidents, he is still pretty low. And if the news related to the Buzzard Creek Tent City massacre is allowed to get out and be legitimised, he might be voted out and replaced by his own party and his Exclusion League backers," Jackson said.

"No kidding," Jennifer said. "Less money for schools and for any program that is designed to elevate everyday people without private recourses. It is like his cult of followers are willing to condemn the unconverted, than to try to see things from their point of view," Jennifer said.

"It is also about community inside the warzones. All creatures including humans need community. Without a sense of community, of any form, people harden. Having a sense of community that includes being socially connected to people who have something in common that they can all relate to, you will see the best in people coming to the surface, without any coercion. Just people being people together in a common grounded setting, electrifies the individual soul with life," Jackson said.

"I thought you did broadcast journalism for the glamour," Jennifer said.

"Partly, I suppose. When I first saw Dianne, in real life, I thought she was the most glamorous woman that I ever met. Every day was like a holiday after I started to work beside Dianne," Jackson replied.

"But didn't you two work in most of the warzones that are having economic impact around the world. How do you stay glamorous in conditions that are so brutal?" Jennifer asked.

"You have to ask Dianne because I don't have a clue how she does it," Jackson said.

Chapter 7

March 21st 2031, around 10:00 AM

"What is wrong, son?" James asked Bobby.

"I don't like robots planning my schedule. I think it should be my job to plan my day," Bobby said.

"Please don't start with how robots are taking over jobs meant for humans. I just had a huge argument with Jackson and Dianne yesterday evening, and I am still exhausted," James said.

"Mina is a lot different than I expected. I fill like I am sticking out instead of fitting in. It almost feels like a person needs to become like a cyborg to stay relevant. How do we compete with robots if we don't become more robotic? Did our side of the pond get frozen in time or something? Here people seem to be interconnected and much friendlier and freer than we are, even the ones living and working in the secretive military zone. As long as they have a scannable chip in their forehead, they seem to be all treated like valued contributors of their society. There are no outcasts sitting on curbs the way there are in Pitville. What I see outside my own center of the universe makes me question everything that I used to believe was my birthright and my true destiny. After my time in the labor camp my eyes were opened and I saw beyond my own fate. It is not just the people of Mina being forced to live behind a wall, but it is all of us being forced to live like that. A wall is a wall, and whatever side you may be living on, it still matters that trade and movement are intentionally being slowed down to a halt, causing a crash. So that President Peel's backers can profit when people are forced to sell their stuff dirt cheap," Bobby said.

"That is why we are here, son, we have left the Dark Ages behind us," James replied.

"Are you sure Dad? Look at those kids, tethered to each other with what looks like a dog leash," Bobby wondered out loud.

"Those children are being socialized to be miners. To work as one for the greater good. Caring about something greater than oneself brings people closer to a higher power, and that is a good thing. Excluding everyone but the elite, creates a selfish population that is stunted through Peel's brainwashing," James explained. "In Mina there is a collective effort to grow food and an economy which sustains everyday people, not just the financial elite.

"Are you sure Dad? I just find it hard to believe that the militarized aspect of all this is not hiding something," Bobby said.

"You mean the way Peel's exclusion league is hiding his true intentions of militarizing the wall?" James asked.

Chapter 8

March 21st 2031, around 11:00 AM

"What is this?" Mayor Stern demanded to know.

"It is our second eviction notice, Sir. We are being evicted from Tut Island," Susan tried to explain.

"Sir, it is awful. Apparently the International United Federation of Nations has determined that Tut Island is stolen territory, and is actually owned by the great people of Mina's Heartland. Obviously the United Federation of Nations is an enemy organization and President Peel have declared another national emergency, and any idle person without employment will be drafted into the Tut People's army and will be issued brown and black uniforms to wear," John Bell, head of security said.

"Hold on is this for real?" Susan asked.

"I thought this accusation of stealing Tut Island was at best a joke, and at worse a ploy from whoever is behind all the fake news that is taking over social media," Mayor Stern said, as he rang the little bell he had resting next to his new gravel. "Rum and coke for everyone," Mayor Stern declared.

"Is this an official refreshment break, or are we going to drink ourselves into oblivion so we can fight this war and new national emergency blind and oblivious to any pain?" Susan asked.

"Susan, please shut up," John and Mayor Stern said at the same time.

"Where is James Coaltonstone? He should be here," Mayor Stern asked.

"I heard that James is testing his new hyperloop rail system while engaging in transcontinental travel," John Bell replied.

"You would think a man of James Coaltonstone's years would be resting," Susan said.

"It is not like James Coaltonstone to go away without a word to anyone," Mayor Stern said.

"I heard that James is actually stocking the mines with fighter bots that are able to bore holes and mine and build underground roads and railways. So he might not be as far away as we think. That new train of his can gets him around at over 600 miles an hour, and he is planning on doubling that speed in the near future," John Bell said.

Where is he? I haven't seen or heard from him for days. And what is President Peel saying about our eviction notice?" Mayor Stern asked.

"Mr. Coaltonstone wasn't scheduled to make a test run in his new hyperloop railway network, but I heard from our spies that he decided to leave early and he may have taken Bobby and Alex with him and they are probably in the militarized zone across the pond, by now," John Bell said.

"And what do your spies say about President Peel's reaction when he was given the eviction notice for the Tut Territory to be handed over to Mina?" Mayor Stern asked.

"I heard that he tore the document up and told the wall builders to add more barbwire to the wall and to add more windmills," John Bell replied.

"And this wall is supposed to do what? Stop us from fleeing?" Susan asked.

"Susan, shut up. All the great cities from the past were fortified," John ordered.

"I don't like you speaking to my secretary like that, and she does have a point, we don't want to be living in the past. We need to be moving towards the future faster than everyone else. James seems to always know how to succeed. He is able to make his dreams come alive, paving a way for his chosen destiny to live and grow without restraints. I just hope he stays in touch," " Mayor Stern said.

"And look at who he tramples on, without concern, conscience or any pretense of restraint. That James Coaltonstone crushes people's dreams, so that he can make his own dreams come alive," Susan said.

"Shut up, Susan," John Bell ordered.

"How many times have I asked you to stop telling Susan to shut up? It is my job to tell Susan to shut up," Mayor Stern said.

"And that is one job a robot hasn't taken from you yet, Sir," Susan replied.

"Susan, Please," Mayor Stern said.

"You tell Susan to shut up all the time," John Bell retorted.

"Yes, but that is different; I am Susan's boss," Mayor Stern said. "And that wall will certainly not stop the Minese from invading us and our territory if they want to. If anything, that wall could make it much harder for us to leave the territory," Mayor Stern said. "Excuse me while I answer the phone, Martha has flagged this call urgent.

"I guess this meeting will be adjourned any many now," Susan said.

"Susan, you don't know that," John Bell replied. "We still have important matters to discuss in regards to the militia and their captives.

"What is wrong Martha? You know I am in an important meeting," Mayor Stern said as he winked at John and Susan.

"What do you mean another bridge has been burned down by homeless people? Are you okay? I will be there right away, dear. Stay locked in the car," Mayor Stern ordered but tried to make his tone of voice sound more of a gentle suggestion.

"Sounds like the revolution is about to begin," Susan said.

"Oh, Susan shut up. It is just those revolting people revolting against authority, putting people at risk and destroying public property, nothing more and nothing less," John said.

"This meeting is now adjourned." Mayor Stern said as he tapped his gravel on his big oak desk.

"Sir, as head of security I feel obligate to tag along. You will need a driver to drive your government car back to City Hall," John Bell said.

"Good plan," Mayor Stern said.

"And we will blaring the siren and flashing the emergency lights as we drive as fast as we safely can," John Bell said.

"And before you go Susan, please shred our notes," Mayor Stern order.

"Certainly Sir," Susan said. "Make sure John drives safely, he can be a maniac at the wheel," Susan said.

"I will be driving the car, thank you very much," Mayor Stern said as he took the keys from John.

Chapter 9

March 21st 2031, around 12:10 PM

"I don't like this," Bobby said.

"No one asked for your opinion," Alex replied.

"These kids are bred and raised to work in these tunnels, regardless of what the tunnels are used for, these tunnels are now their home. They know no other life," James explained.

"So what do we call them? Child soldiers?" Bobby asked.

"Of course, not. They are miners. They are people who are privilege to have food and water security and a safe place to sleep at night. They have a lot more than the miners we left behind in Pitville who are technically homeless and are treated as transients without any residential connections to the town they spent most of their lives. Now they are treated like data points on a graph stigmatized as hobos. These kids are better off that. We all are. We are moving products and workers faster than any other operation. Our hyperloop network is going to revolutionize mobility the way cell phones revolutionized communication. It will be like floating on air towards the future, faster than anyone else," Alex said.

"It is time for our own revolution. That President Peel mocks my country, laughs at our National Anthem, manipulates markets that bring famine to my people, and puts up ugly walls in beautiful places. We are extracting what we can under the wall for a greater purpose. We will bore through hundreds if not thousands of feet, and free the wealth underneath. We can build a thriving community, where all working people are treated fairly. We will thrive, while hiding right under Tut metropolis and Tut Territorial Islands. If there are any rumbles, they will assume they are just minor earthquakes.

The hyperloop train can take us a thousand miles in a couple of hours. No one will get ahead of us. Not even President Peel and his Exclusion League backers," Ono said.

Chapter 10

March 21st 2031, around 12:10 PM

Of course we are winning the revolution," James said. "As long as we control the land, the Heartland, we have won. Wars are always won that way. President Peel does not know the land the way I and my colleagues know the land, isn't that right Ono?"

"Completely. We have always controlled the land whereas the westerners control the routes to our land," Ono replied.

"Well, all that is changing, because we have the machines to bore tunnels to provide access to my hyperloop train network, which will connect the all land, even the land under the sea," James said.

"And we survivalists, James. All of our people find ways to survive, and we allow them the freedom to so. We have survival vending markets, where people can exchange items and maybe it is not the best way, but in your land, what happens to all those displaced people? They are hunted down, as if social cleansing was a moral duty of the super-rich and their cronies. In our land we really network, we really work together, because we have to. People defend the motherland because they are defending themselves and their brothers, sisters, elderly parents and children. The people here, are the social net that catches those who fall between the cracks. In your land what happens to the displaced people. They become statistics, to be analyzed as if they were mere data points.

"Have you seen a white boy, his name is Mathew, who may have been wearing a flyking suit. He was shot down, by a couple of fools, my company erroneously hired, assuming he was a drone, or they may have shot him down because he had been taking photographs and was mistaken for a spy. Have you seen him or heard of his whereabouts?" James asked.

"No, I haven't been informed of any white boys being arrested in the military zone," Ono said.

"He is my step-son," James replied.

"I will look into it, James. Who knows, he could have been hidden somewhere by the young blood hunters, especially if he has O negative blood," Ono promised.

We actually found four of your freeman miners passed out in the shipment that you sent us. We killed the one called Sam, but the other three, Kevin, George and Jay, managed to escape. We believe they may have escaped into our commuter tunnels, some of those are connected to yours. We allow our people to move through those tunnels freely in order to keep our economy vibrant and fast moving. Once our economy slows down, just like yours, it could crash, even faster than yours. Our tunnel system is directly connected to Heartland and to the many survival vendors' markets that keep our economy alive. Maybe we are not using the greatest economic model in the world, but who needs a great economic model that just works in theory? Our communal economic theories will probably be blamed when the global economy collapses. The trade between nations is more important for Tut Territory than for Mina and the Heartland. Once this great trade war grinds Tut Island's economy to a halt, many buried skeletons will be in full sight to haunt President Peel and his Exclusion League backers. The injustices the Minese have endured as a people, for the last century will be fully exposed. Once trade between nations comes to a full stop we will be blamed and those tariffs, counter tariffs and border closings, which are creating so much investor uncertainty will continue," Ono said.

"You think your country will be blamed for the collapse of the global economy?" James asked.

"You think we won't be blamed?" Ono asked as his reply, as they both puffed on Cuban cigars.

"I can see your point, Ono," James said as he made smoke rings.

"History proves that fanaticism doesn't need logic, all it needs is an enemy, someone to hate so that this hate can dominate the thinking process of the masses," Ono said.

"I am facing uncertainty myself," James said.

"The only certainty there is, is the need for revolution before this mad man starves us all to death," Ono replied.

"People are afraid to invest in anything that can be exchanged for goods and services," James said.

"We prefer to be focusing on food security since food is what keeps us alive, and as long as we stay alive, the revolution lives. President Peel prefers his tariffs of death, to force his enemies into submission," Ono said.

"Tell me about it," James said.

"President Peel is missing the point that his currency contributes to people buying imported and survival market goods from us cause of our lower valued currency. Whenever that President Peel attacks us with unfair tariffs which are supposed to assassinate our markets, our currency gets devalued, then the Tut Territory currency gets overvalued and our goods are even cheaper for consumers than buying locally in the Tut Territory," Ono said.

"Try telling him that," James said.

"That is why we must have a revolution. The man's biases are born out of privilege and continues to perverse class struggle, that I am destined to win. President Peel goes on about making the Tut Territory great again, but he isn't improving quality of life for ordinary people, and this how I will win. He is just making life great for himself and his capitalist cronies. One day I will become the most power general in history. I must free the working class from the tyranny on all the external demands that are being imposed on their labor.

Demands which never benefit the laborers, but only lead to hunger and a premature death," Ono said.

"I have never been comfortable with President Peel's and the Exclusion League's social cleansing policies. Only a mad man would believe that social cleansing could be imposed on the people without violence," James said.

"Isn't the power of hate, a form of violence, towards our national soul? Connecting to our national soul energizes our collective life, and our conscience validates our humanity to each other. We live in a country where we are free to follow our dream as a nation, beyond borders and beyond walls. Those dreams of self-determined destiny will inspire our nation to greatness, in the same way other nations are inspired to greatness. On the other hand, fate seals our national outcome, resulting in lowered expectations and food insecurity. We export our people to foreign masters while our natural resources are used as weapons against us. No wonder we feel as if we are a conquered nation," Ono said.

"I am here to help you take control back. Same thing could be said for the Territory of Tut. Who in their right mind threatens to shut down their country while closing their nation's borders to trade and tourism? Sure a few bad apples get in, but most people I have come across, are good people. Who is willing to shut down the country's government, and threaten to close borders to vital economic two way traffic, in my opinion is insane, And the total shut down of a country's borders without concern for the country's food security, is criminal negligence," James shouted.

"Food security is everything. Without food security the people will be too weak to climb walls and to fight back," Ono said.

"Exactly," James said.

"Fanaticism does not feed the people's bodies. And it is the people's bodies that fight the revolution. You cannot win a revolution based on negative bias, alone. The Heartland can feed the force of revolution. A country without food security is doomed. And the doomed are not free to dream the impossible or feel inspired enough to create their own destiny. If we allow ourselves to be forced into serving foreign masters we will seal our fate and lose control over our own future. A great nation cannot give up its own food security by closing the border to the Heartland. Such an act will doom a nation into starvation. President Peel will be known to be one of the greatest fools I history, because he fools himself, and his people allow him to act the fool. His negative bias dominates every decision he makes while feeding working class pessimism. I watch from afar as I see President Peel, trapping the working class in typical push and pull negative loops that only energize and benefit the master forces with limitless profit generated from continuous warfare and conflicts. President Peel as his Exclusion League cronies are just as much victim of his negative biases as we are. He feels the continuous pull growing from the culture he was raised in. He never questioned the negative biases because those prejudices empowered him and it is that power that justifies excluding and dehumanizing us while making his own administration just as unsustainable as that silly wall that my people will breach and break into a million pieces. We will take no prisoners and we will burn the fat of our stolen land to generate power. We have our observation deck and mining facilities hidden on the far side of the moon. We do this, while that silly President Peel is spending billions on a wall that we are destined to crush," Ono said as he made smoke rings from the cigar James Coaltonstone had gifted him.

CHAPTER 11

March 21st 2031, around 2:30 PM

"You, my great followers, are never fooled by all that fake news that comes from Mina or for that matter, from the PPZ hiding over there in the press gallery," President Peel said.

"And you think that the world hasn't gone insane?" Jennifer whispered to Jackson.

"I definitely do. As we stand here watching this spectacle called a political rally, it is self-evident the world has been taken over by mad men," Jackson replied. "Hold on I am getting a call, it is a conference call from the Coaltonstones."

"Jackson I read your new blog, and I am disputing the rumors that you and your fake press cohorts are insinuating. If there was a massacre a couple of nights ago, I had nothing to do with it. I have been out of town, and I am planning to stay out of town for a while. I would like to see the evidence first, or I will be seeing you in court. I am also disputing the rumors that the fake press are making relating to Coalton Two. My new town is recovering from the rockslide and is doing a lot more than just existing. And Coalton Two will still exist, even after we are all gone, because my business model is sustainable. My bots continue to mine coal because they work under extreme heat and filth 24 hours a day and seven days a week. And my human team..." James began before Jackson interrupted.

"You mean your prisoners, many of them are minors," Jackson said.

"They are miners," James retorted.

"I mean minor miners, as in under age. You know James, this is an inappropriate place to be discussing this matter. I am at one of President Peel's rallies, and the rally is getting crazy," Jackson explained.

"If I say this is the right time to discuss your blog, then it is the right time, or I will be discussing it with you in court. My crew were born and raised to mine. That is all they know and want to know. The younger miners are able to fit into places my bots cannot fit into. Their fate was sealed by circumstances before they were born. Look at President Peel inciting violence towards the Minese. That is the stigma which condemning them, not me. And I offer them food security, which they have never known before and will never know again, they will follow me like dogs," James said.

"I see that Jennifer is with you and Dianne. I must tell her something, and I know this is not the right place, but we found Mathew," Alex said.

"I wanted to tell her," Bobby retorted.

"As the head of the household I was the one who was supposed to tell her," James argued back.

"Jennifer, Mathew is still in the Minese military zone prison, and we are trying to get him back home without creating an international incident," James explained.

"You found him? He is in a prison? Is he hurt? I can't believe it. I feel like a black cloud that was floating over my head has just disappeared. Is someone going to tell me what happened? How is he? Is he okay? Will I recognize him?" Jennifer asked.

"Ono found him," Alex said. "And we don't know much more than that."

"You mean they won't tell you much more?" Jennifer replied.

"Exactly," Alex said. "We haven't even seen him yet. We just talked to him over the phone."

"Mathew said that he loved you very much," Bobby interjected.

"And why are we even trading with those people who are so willing to hold children, against their will?" Jackson asked. "I thought we are at war with them."

"Because Mina controls the Heartland which is not only one of the major bread baskets of the world but also has one of the greatest supply of energy, which could fuel the engines of this world for decades to come," James replied.

"Now you are all for stopping war and world hunger? I wonder what the unintended results will be."

'You have never felt food insecurity, have you Jackson? I see it every day. A person who hasn't seen others experiencing that constant hunger has no idea what it is like. How hunger is able to stunt an entire nation's growth and development. It is an act of war when one nation stunts another nation's development by sabotaging their food source," James said.

"I have been to plenty of warzones in my day where farmland and forests were intentionally poisoned. I have seen what hunger does to people. I have seen how hunger destroys civility between people who used to be best of friends," Jackson retorted.

"I see how President Peel has intentionally assassinated my markets and then acts innocent and clueless when my mines have to close and hunger and homelessness displaces so many hard working people. I will not let that man put a seal on my fate the way he has for so many others. No one should assume the authority and power to stunt another human being. We will not be forced into reduced circumstances or allow that fool to wall us in as if he were the only master of fate. I too am a master of fate, and certainly the master of my own destiny," James said.

"But, James, don't you seal people's fate too? And what about Wednesday night's massacre? Maybe you don't hurt people for political advantage but who do you put first, the people or profit?" Jackson asked.

"If there was a massacre, and we don't know that yet, I had nothing to do with it. Maybe you don't like my methods, but at least I am giving the crews of illegals food security and a safe place to be. Things some have them have never experienced before and may never experience again. Peel's policies are silently starving the people of the Tut territory. Thousands of people are dying on the streets. He is deliberately starving people out of existence. At least I am offering food security in return for labor and that offer will win me the election," James said.

"You contribute to all this craziness too. You will do anything to finance your hyperloop rail network and finance all those tunnels that you are boring into. It is amazing the ground above some of those tunnels hasn't collapsed yet," Jackson said.

"That is what makes me great. I am able to make things work. I am renting my team out to the state so that labor intensive work can get done, because my crewmembers are great. If I did not rent out these chain gangs someone else would be, and their crew would not be as great as my crew. My teams are rented out to all kinds of organizations to mine and as extract minerals from the ground. And as we extract all those minerals we create and enforce tunnels for transport, and Ono's debt retrieval services," James said.

"How do you live with all these terrible contradictions? You must know you can't take all of your material wealth with you. The Big Seven Coal Group defines how social control defies quality control. You are just as mad as President Peel, maybe even worse. You say how great you are going to make things if you win the next election, but how can you make things great for us when you leave nothing for the people you exploit and whose labor has built your empire? You don't even have to pay them. And whatever happened to those 4 miners that went down Mine Five to help rescue Ginger Goodwin? George, Jay, Sam and Kevin, whatever happened to them," Jackson asked.

"I have no idea. Lots of people have left Pitville once the work dried up. I have done nothing that no one else would have not done if given a chance. The real question is how does President Peel get away with assassinating my markets? How does he think he will be getting away with assassinating markets that he and this country are actually indebted to? Sure I rent out my crews to rake the brush in the forests. I was given possession of the crewmembers when President Peel declared them to be illegals. Before that we just treated them as undocumented workers. Their forced servitude, is not my responsibility. It is how they repay their debt to society. Some of the crew arrived undocumented while travelling back and forth between the Tut Territory and Mina, others were just born undocumented. Is that my fault that they do not legally exist as a person, and never will? To be undocumented and is the same as being condemned to a non-existence and having no personhood. I cannot change such a cruel fate, unless I become president, of course. With all that said, President Peel is in charge of the great territory of Tut and is a firm believer that raking forests is a viable, sustainable and sensible way to prevent forest fires. These undocumented workers, illegals as President Peel would call them, are easily imported and exported. No one reports them to be officially missing, because technically they don't exist, the way you and I exist," James explained. "How can anyone report a missing person when they have never existed?"

"What?" Jackson replied back.

"My job is to provide workers as needed. And my transcontinental hyperloop rail service will do the job in hours, instead of days. We will put an end to forest fires before you know it. I have the technology and know-how to import and export able-bodied workers to do any kind of labor intensive and dirty job as required. My workers have been trained from infancy to obey orders because they know their true boss is the one who is willing to feed them for an honest day's work," James said. "My crews will be collecting fallen leaves from our great forests because only we can prevent forest fires. We and my crew will bring back the heart to the Heartland.

"And you think this plan will really prevent forest fires and bring back the heart in the Heartland?" Jackson asked.

"I think James just likes shouting at us," Dianne interjected.

"That is not true Dianne. We are doers, you know that. We are building new trade routes to connect Eurasia with

North America. We have the crews and we have the drive to fuel the engines of this world and President Peel believes that raking leaves, with slave labor, if we must call the crews that, will prevent forest fires, economically. If the people don't have jobs, then they have lost their relevancy, and whose fault is that? Jobs bring back relevancy and will make the Tut Territory great again," James said.

"Isn't that what slave-owners said when they forced millions into slavery and forced servitude the last time?" Jackson interjected a little louder than he meant to.

"So what, Jackson. Greatness does not happen when my markets are being assassinated, to keep small elites financially privileged. We should not have to be suffering like this or fear crime, bad air quality or smoky sidewalks or see brown gunk come out of our taps whenever it rains the water pollution that seems to appear every time it rains," James shouted.

"And what are you going to do about that black cloud over Pitville or the broken mountain in Coalton Two. You are the most accident prone industrialist that I have ever met," Jackson shouted back. And adding to all this suffering, you took houses away from your workers in Pitville and condemned them to homelessness," Jackson shouted back.

"I own those houses. Those houses were no longer housing miners in Pitville so I sent them to Coalton Two, to house my crew. My crew will be living underground, we will be travelling underground, and one day we will be the directors of the great Heartland above ground," James said. "All I ever wanted to do was build an empire that could grow beyond the walls that mediocre men use to socially engineer their own, selfish success. I have always wanted to make the world a better place, for all different classes of people, who, when working together, are able to make the world great, not just through competition, but through co-operation. All I ever wanted to do was to expand and improve my ability to import and export my growing lines of products, and to fuel the engines of the world. I have always wanted to be free from the confines of mediocre men like President Peel who puff themselves up by abusing their own discretionary power. I want to be free of the man whose tariffs, counter tariffs and walls are designed to stifle the greatness of others. President Peel is using his archaic tariffs to assassinate my markets and to socially engineer his own success. He gives his cronies a much needed advantage over my ingenuity that is second to none while inflating prices. I don't want anyone to get hurt," James shouted.

"Now you are calling your slaves people," Jackson shouted back to James.

"You people over there in the press gallery, please shut up. You are interrupting my rally with all the noise you are making," President Peel ordered.

"Hey morons, President Peel told you to sit down. Hey aren't you Jackson Green and Dianne Black from the PPZ?

"Yes, we are, and I am on an important conference call," Jackson replied.

"You are just a PPZ cameraman from Fake News Inc.," the burly man said as he pushed Jackson to the ground.

Another burly men joined in the commotion and another pulled out a knife, and stuck it into Jackson's abdomen as Jackson yelled out an ear-piercing scream, the burly man took out the knife and then stuck it into Dianne's abdomen before it broke.

"Jackson! Dianne!" Jennifer screamed out, as both Dianne and Jackson fell to the ground.

"Arrest that man. He just stabbed the reporter and cameraman from PPZ, live on TV. Arrest that fool and anyone that gets in the way. I don't care if they are related to Major Bell of Tut Territory Homeland Security or if they are related to the King of England. I am the president and I am the one giving out orders. Arrest them!" President Peel screamed.

"Hell, you keep telling us that the PPZ couple, Jackson Green and Dianne Black, are enemies of the people," another burly man standing in the boisterous crowd yelled back.

"Arrest that man too," President Peel yelled at the top of his voice as his face turned a bright orangy-red.

"What is going on over there? Why is everyone shouting? I can't hear myself think," James asked as he shouted through his phone.

"Mr. Coaltonstone, this is Jennifer Jones. Jackson and Dianne have been stabbed really badly. I put you on the speaker phone because I am trying to keep them warm and trying to stop the bleeding until help arrives," Jennifer said.

CHAPTER 12

March 21st 2031, around 2:45 PM

"Mr. Coaltonstone, Jackson and Dianne are really hurt, I have no idea what to do" Jennifer said as she began to cry.

"Open up their shirts and see how bad their wounds are," James interjected.

"Mr. Coaltonstone, I can't do that," Jennifer protested.

"You must," James ordered.

"Go ahead," Dianne said. "Jackson won't mind especially if he is hurting as much as I am."

"You wouldn't believe how bad this hurts. This is not the way I want to die. I wanted to live a bit like a family man, you know, have a nice garden, a nice car outside my nice house, living with my beautiful wife and surrounded by my loving and adoring children. I am so fed up with being in warzone after warzone, disaster zone after disaster zone and conflict after conflict. Pitville never had to get this bad," Jackson replied.

"Mr. Coaltonstone, they are both bleeding from their abdomens. Jackson is sounding delirious, as if his entire life is passing him by. I have opened up Dianne's shirt and oh my God, part of the knife is still in Dianne's stomach. I have put my coat over Dianne. I am now opening up Jackson's shirt. There is something bulging from Jackson's abdomen," Jennifer screamed into the phone.

"I hurt so much. I think that is my bowel sticking out," Jackson.

"Didn't you take this job for the glamour, Jackson, besides opportunity to travel the world and meet the movers and shakers?" Dianne asked.

"You bet, Di, nothing gets more glamorous than this. For once people are photographing me, as much as you. Today might be the final day of my life, and I had no idea when I woke up this morning, or I would have stayed in bed," Jackson replied.

"Me too, I would have stayed in bed, if I knew this was going to happen," Dianne said.

"It is okay Jackson, Mr. Coaltonstone is going to get help for us. I am going to put my sweater under your head to make you more comfortable," Jennifer said.

"Jackson, I don't want to die like this. I want the same things you want and I want to share them with you. To have a family and life that is free from war, conflict and fear. I think we are going to die before we actually lived. I hurt like you wouldn't believe, I have so many regrets," Dianne said.

"I needed this hole in my abdomen like I needed a hole in my head," Jackson said and began to laugh.

"Don't touch it, just leave it. I am going to get some really qualified help for you two. Hold on to your hats," James interjected.

"I just got blood on my hands," Jennifer said.

"Now you have something in common with President Peel," Jackson said and then started to giggle uncontrollably.

"I need to get off the phone and try to do something to help them. No one is helping us. People are just circling around us and making videos with their phones. They are moving back and forth, zooming in with their feet, from different angles, while Jackson and Dianne are lying on the ground bleeding to death. They are losing blood, not a lot that I can see. They are both pale and sweating," Jennifer said as she tried to stay calm.

"They are probably bleeding from inside their abdomens. Why did you even go to one of those horrible President Peel's rally? You know how people get all wound up at those rallies and do crazy things impulsively," James said.

"I went with Dianne and Jackson because it is technically an important public event, and it should be safe, and they were assigned to film it for a live PPZ broadcast, and I was going to get credit from Tut high for participating in civics," Jennifer replied.

"You mean Jackson and Dianne were stabbed, live on international TV?" James asked.

"Yes, and crowds of people are turning up here, pointing their cameras at us. And no one is helping us," Jennifer replied.

"I just hope the fake news doesn't start blaming me for this too. They are still blaming me for the black clouds that lurk over Pitville and Coalton Two. And they blame me for the Cold Feet Mountain rock slide, as if I would plan such a horrible disaster," James said defensively.

"Mr. Coaltonstone, I am not blaming you for anything at all, but I need to get off the phone. This is so horrible. There is a huge mob gathering around us. There must be at least a a a thousand people now or maybe even more. They are just standing around us making videos and looking like blood thirsty zombies, no one is helping us," Jennifer said. "I really hope you can help us and help Mathew too. I would be in your debt for the rest of my life, if you could help us," Jennifer pleaded.

"I will bring Mathew home, dear. And you will owe me nothing. I am going to see what I can do to help Jackson and Dianne, from over here, where there is a lot less chaos. I blame everyone involved in the stabling. They lack discipline to maintain enough objectivity to remember the difference between right and wrong, so technically they could claim insanity and for that matter President Peel could too."

"Mr. Coaltonstone, I need to hang up now and help Jackson and Dianne. You would not believe how badly hurt they are. I think they are dying, all these people are just taking videos of us and I feel like screaming at them," Jennifer said.

"Just stay calm, dear. I am going to get things moving to help Dianne and Jackson. I am sure Dianne is doing her best, but President Peel could be sabotaging her efforts. Dianne loves Jackson very much, she won't let him die, if she can help it and neither will I. And I won't let Mathew be forgotten either. I can just imagine how chaotic it must be over there. I hate those rallies," James replied.

"Mr. Coaltonstone, they are sweating and turning really pale. I have blood all over my hands. Jackson and Dianne are suffering from terrible pain. I really have to go. Promise me you won't let Mathew fall through the cracks and be turned into just another irrelevant, missing kid," Jennifer pleaded.

"I will try my best. I love Mathew too, you know, in my own way. You ask Jackson to tell you and Dianne the story about Deep Coal. That should keep both of them awake until help arrives. Goodbye dear," James said.

"Goodbye, Mr. Coaltonstone," Jennifer replied.

"Mr. Green, Mr. Coaltonstone told me to ask you about Deep Coal. You are supposed to tell it to us, so you keep yourself and Dianne awake. Mr. Coaltonstone said he is going to get really good help for us," Jennifer said.

"I heard everything he said. That man never speaks without shouting," Dianne said.

"President Peel never speaks without shouting either. I don't know who shouts more, President Peel or James Coaltonstone. I will tell you something, Jennifer, I am Deep Coal," Jackson whispered in Jennifer's ear, and don't tell Di" Jackson said.

"I don't know who Deep Coal is," Jennifer admitted. "You are bleeding heavily. I wish someone would help us. Why can't someone help us?" Jennifer screamed.

"I suppose in the end, fate throws us all hardballs, to test our resilience," Jackson said struggling for breath. "Life on this planet must have been just a test. I see so much light. I am not prepared for the next level of existence. I never believed that there was another level of existence, but maybe there is. I wasn't really prepared for my life on Earth either, but the more I became aware, the more I felt my own existence. It all just seemed to happen," Jackson said, while Jennifer, still holding Jackson's phone, was trying to make Jackson and Dianne more comfortable, while she started to cry, while sitting in a growing pool of Jackson's blood.

"Jennifer, everything is going to be okay. You won't be alone all your life, Mathew will be back by your side, one day soon," Jackson said.

"No, you are not, Why doesn't someone help us?" Jennifer screamed again.

"No one wants to get involved. Crowds watching disaster, accidents and train wrecks are all like that. I want to tell you something, Jennifer, as long as you are living, make your own second chances because no one will give them you. This terrible conflict will only encourage more disdain for human life. Bare witness to these terrible times, and then maybe one day, the life we used to know, will return," Jackson said.

"Jennifer don't ever forget your passion, for it can energize you and empower you to ignore your own fears so you can continue to follow your dreams and your destiny. Do what you and Mathew were born to do, even Mathew can't be at your side. You observe what exists because there will be a path which leads to destinies, good ones and bad ones. Existence is what is, but destiny is the end of the journey. I just assumed my destiny would be different than dying like this, lying on the ground in all this chaos, maybe even drowning in my own blood," Jackson said.

"We are not dying Jackson. We can't die. We have our kids to look after. We have the world to change. We have our fans," Dianne said.

"Fans? Where are our fans now? Just said it Di, We have been abandoned," Jackson said.

"I am here, I won't abandon either of you," Jennifer said as she tried to comfort them.

"Jennifer, if you must avenge us, do not cause harm. Just care as much as we do," Jackson said.

"We will recover from this. And our recovery will bare witness to how we persevere through adversity while ignoring our fear. People who have lowered themselves into a mob mentality are often very irrational," Dianne interjected.

"Remember it is not just about us. It is about the human suffering that should never be happening, but must be recorded, so that we learn from history and change the direction fate is heading. Following our dreams instead of running away from what scares us, changes who we are and who we can be. Our destiny is in our hands. Destiny can make and break us, especially if society collapses all around us," Jackson said.

"If society collapses? Don't you mean when?" Dianne interjected again.

"I think you two need to calm down though Mr. Coaltonstone said you shouldn't fall asleep," Jennifer said.

"Do we sound like we are falling asleep?" Dianne asked.

"I feel so weak. I never felt this weak before. Always remember Jennifer avenging for harm done, the harm grows when more harm is done to others. The destructive culture of the Exclusion League and the Brotherhood is just looking for excuses to lash out at others," Jackson said.

"The worse thing is all the panic the violence causes. And when people panic they never seem to act rationally," Dianne said.

"Yeah, everyone who found themselves stuck in the warzones seemed to follow the same narrative," Jackson said.

"And then there were those horribly lumpy beds," Dianne said.

"And we were lucky to have beds," Jackson said.

"The more sleep deprived and hungry people grew, the more violent people became," Dianne said.

"You know, one thing I noticed about you and Mathew, is how gentle you two are. I always guessed that you were so gentle because you spend so much time photographing nature's natural beauty," Jackson said.

"And look at where Mathew is now. He made himself vulnerable because he was flyking and photographing in warzone. Everywhere is a warzone now. Jethro and Bill and their crewmates can technically shoot anyone with a camera and call them a spy. The more I think about the more I am sure when he was shot down, he fell on the other side of the wall, and now he is captive somewhere in Mina. And that is the best scenario. No one knows for sure where Mathew is exactly, what state he is in, or anything," Jennifer said.

"Some people believe beauty is worth dying for," Jackson said.

"Mathew is not dead," Jennifer said in protest.

"What Jackson means is beauty is something people are willing to protect, even with their life. Pitville was very beautiful at one time," Dianne said.

"And they destroyed the beauty around them to elevate themselves from poverty. And where are they now? Worse off than they were before. As they extracted what they could, exploited what they could, they destroyed the beauty that surrounded them. We assume that their slavery doesn't exist. We were all meant to be free and to feel relevant in our existence. Everyone needs a way out from the tunnels below into the world above. You are now my eyes. You search for truth. You enter the warzone, capture what you can, while dodging bullets and bombs. I never thought I would die at a rally held by my president. If anything I thought I would in a warzone in some foreign land," Jackson said.

"You are not going to die here, I won't let you. Mr. Coaltonstone promised that he would get the best help he could," Jennifer said.

"We all have to die sometime. You avenge us by collecting evidence. You avenge us by not letting truth be invisible. Just the way Mathew did. And remember, as long as you have evidence of existence, there is proof of your existence too, that will survive, even when we are gone. Don't let that President Peel, and his double talk mix you up. And forgive me for making people think that it was Ginger Goodwin who was Deep Coal, because it was me, I was Deep Coal. We all have the right to exist. You do, Mathew does and Deep Coal, in its own way, does too," Jackson said.

"Mr. Coaltonstone promised me he will help Mathew and get someone to help you, so you must hold on," Jennifer said.

"You were Deep Coal?" Dianne asked as she winced in pain.

"You two must calm down. You will make the bleeding worse. Mr. Coaltonstone said he would get help," Jennifer said.

"Wherever James Coaltonstone goes, disaster follows. I won't be holding my breath waiting for James Coaltonstone to help anyone but himself. I know they told us Mathew is alive. And we are too. But look at us. Hopefully Mathew is in better shape than we are in. Jackson, you promised me that you knew nothing about Deep Coal's identity," Dianne said.

"You guys need to stay calm. I will be so grateful when Mathew is back here with me. It will be like nothing has changed. I am never going to give up on Mathew. I just know he will be back with me, soon. Jackson, Di, don't give up wither. Keep holding on to your life here. Mr. Coaltonstone said that he is getting help. You both have to survive this. You have to get better for the children's sake. We all need you to tell us and to show us the truth. We all need you to stay strong," Jennifer said.

"When Mathew comes home, he will need you to accept him for who he is now, who he has become," Jackson said.

"Of course I will love him, in the same way I always have. Nothing is going to change that. Whatever Mathew is doing to survive, I would support 100 percent. If we believe and try hard enough we will be able to overcome all this cruelty and injustice, without becoming cruel and unjust ourselves," Jennifer said.

"I used to believe that too, when I was younger. Now, that I am older, and never being so close to being on my deathbed, or death ground, I don't know if it is even possible to maintain personal integrity and still win," Jackson said.

If you hold onto your ideals, you face a life of poverty, which destroys so many people," Jackson said.

"That is why so many people sell out to the system, even though becoming a member of the Exclusion League has its perks, it is still in many ways a closed and secret society, and dissidents could be hunted down, before they talk. Or at least they are put on the black list," Dianne said.

"They may earn financial rewards, but what do they have in the end when they have denied their conscience? In the end, all that a person will be left with, is their soul. After a lifetime of denying their conscience, the realization that they wasted their life will leave them with a horrible feeling of regret. There is nothing worse than sinking into the abyss of darkness, pain and loneliness. Who are the victims of corruption anyway? The people turned into wards of the state so that they can be exploited and worked to death, out of sight, chained to each other in chain gangs in the mines below our feet? Or their children locked in cages and neglected, left to wonder what they did to deserve such a fate? The law allows the Exclusion League to do whatever they want to do. People are making deals so they can empower and enrich themselves in a world where only the very few have much of anything, anymore. Look at us, we tried so hard to show and tell the truth, and we were attacked today by a fanatic. Being called fake news really hurts. I really don't know what hurts the most. My gut is killing me and I feel like my soul is fading away. I feel so weak, and all my words want out, before I die," Jackson said.

"Jackson, hold on, help will arrive soon. Mr. Coaltonstone promised that he would get help," Jennifer said.

"That horrible weak, dizzy feeling happens when your blood pressure lowers as you lose your blood," Dianne said.

"How do you know that?" Jackson asked

"Because I am feeling the same way," Dianne replied.

"I feel this mushy thing bulging from my gut," Jackson said.

"Stop poking at it, it looks like it could be your bowel," Jennifer said.

"Oh my God," Dianne said.

"I am not ready to die," Jackson said.

"We are not ready to let you die," Jennifer said.

"I think part of the knife broke and is still stuck in my gut, so that might be why I haven't bled to death yet. Thank God for small mercies," Dianne said.

"Who breaks a knife when they stab someone? That guy was totally nuts," Jackson said.

"All you tried to do was show and tell the truth to fanatics, who want to believe that they too can live a life of luxury and greatness the way President Peel does." Jennifer said.

"No one can take any of this stuff with them when they go. There is something really wrong with people, spiritually, who process other humans into beasts of burden, and think nothing of flaunting the wealth that they earned from such a dehumanizing process," Jackson said.

"I hope that did not happen to Mathew. He must be over his head in something he has no control over," Jennifer said.

"Your instincts, if you listen to them, will grow the very destiny that you will feel one with a destiny that makes you more human since you are able to reach your human potential. Once you find that path, follow it for the rest of your life. You will then be able to achieve things way beyond what the Exclusion League will allow outsiders like us to achieve. Your destiny will leave a legacy and the evidence of your existence will be what you were. How you lived in this world will be pave a path for others, for future generations, which may one day be freed by the truth. Maybe we will meet in the next world, if there is one," Jackson said.

"Maybe we will get wings?" Dianne said.

"Come on you two, you don't have to die to fly, all you need is a safety certified flyking suit and permit," Jennifer said.

"Di, promise me, if we recover from this, we can go flyking together and have a picnic somewhere," Jackson said.

"I do, I will, and Jackson we are going to get over this, together. Dying like this, can't be our destiny. We can't give up without a fight, Jackson, We can't let those thugs make us die like this," Dianne said.

"Look around us, do these people look happy? They look like they are a conquered people craving approval from their master," Jennifer said.

"You always see the good in others, Jennifer, these people chose to be dominated by President Peel's authoritarian regime. Destiny can be chosen over fate, but only if you follow your dreams. Even when you are being told otherwise, a fact is a fact. I always cared about the truth data could reveal, because the truth is a physical force. Visible or not, truth creates a direction that we are moving towards and that is why I let Deep Coal grow into what it became. I gave Deep Coal a voice," Jackson said.

"I can't believe that you were Deep Coal. I just assumed that Ginger Goodwin was Deep Coal," Dianne interjected.

"Ginger might have been Deep Coal if he had lived long enough. The data was there and the truth in the data was being suppressed. Deep Coal was the liberating force begging for freedom, like we all do. The data that Ginger had been mining needed Deep Coal's voice, and if not in human form, at least in bot form," Jackson replied.

"You followed your conscience, and that matters," Jennifer said.

"I couldn't stand being a prisoner of my own conscience. I hear self-awareness is the last part of you to die. I feel like I am being pulled away. It feels like I am trapped in a vacuum, and I am just a speck, so much weaker than the force is that is sucking me in," Jackson said.

"Damn you Jackson, don't die without a fight," Dianne ordered.

"Everything you have ever believed in all your life, and your right to record our reality as it plays out, day to day, for future generations to know the truth can't be done if you fade away and die. Don't fall asleep on us, now," Dianne pleaded as she walked into the room. Help is on the way.

"How can destiny be any different than fate, if we don't make a conscious effort to shape our own destiny and follow our dreams?" Jackson asked. "It all seems so dark and empty without these specks off light I see in the distance," Jackson added as he started to gurgle.

"Your existence matters to me, it matters to Di. And your existence will have a huge impact on Mary and David who depend on you, to give them a better life than what they would have had, without you. You are their dad," Jennifer said.

"I am back. They said the medics will be here as soon as they can. I told them it was an emergency," Dianne said. "Don't fade away Jackson. I can't imagine life without you. And what about all of our fans?" Dianne said.

"Our fans? They are your fans, Di. All these people that are surrounding us, taking videos of this, they are not fans, they are fanatics. You are the beautiful one they watch. Sometimes I wonder if they even care about the truth, or my photography and videos. Those very things that we are so prepared to fight and risk our lives for," Jackson said.

"Of course our fans matter, but truth matters even more. As you said, truth is a physical force, it dictates our direction as a species. How could our fans see me, or see the places that we were filming from, if you weren't there holding the camera, dodging bullets, in front of me? You silly twit. We are a team. And you can't quit on me now," Dianne said as she begged Jackson to stay alive.

"It seems all they want to do is look at you. Is the truth that is worth dying for? These people don't seem to know the difference between propaganda and a physical truth. Know one is showing them how to weigh the checks and balances so they can tell what is real from what is fake. I am so weak. I feel like I am fading away. Continue to fight for the truth, Di, you too Jennifer," Jackson whispered as Dianne held his hand.

"Your fans care, Di cares, I care. We are the ones who owe you for protecting our freedom of information, the freedom to know and the freedom of the press. You give us courage to question the thugs who scare us half to death, and try to convince us that it is in our best interest to give up our right to exist and to enjoy life," Jennifer said.

"It is ironic isn't it? We are told to give up who we and deny our soul's longing to be free. And then we are ordered to look fully alive. That is why truth sets us free, because truth is real. Once you realize that you have been deceived, anger can take over, and we lose our peace of mind. We feel it in our soul. The soul feels the truth and for the soul, truth is everything. Why do people lie to us anyway?" Jackson asked.

"My theory is, they are either hiding some big secret, or they are puffing themselves up as a superior over their victims. I suppose negativity gives mediocre people power over other people's minds and traps their opposition, especially their intellectual superiors, in mind-wars," Jennifer said.

"That is another reason why truth sets us free. It gives us a reason to be brave and when we are brave, we feel stronger and freer," Jackson," said.

"Jackson don't fall asleep," Jennifer pleaded.

"We all have the right not to be assaulted but our rights never seem to matter anymore" Jackson said as his voice grew weaker.

"If this the last thing I ever say, always question the lie, Jennifer, so you can stay in touch with your true identity and reach the destiny which is yours. That is your power and that is my power. Even when we are put on the Blacklist, we still must live true to ourselves. Our power scares people who are hiding the truth. President Peel should not be the only one allowed to be the creator of fate and destiny. He should not be the only one in charge of shaping the world's fate for his own benefit. We should all have to right to freedom and happiness and the right to create our own destiny and to follow our dreams, free from obstruction," Jackson said.

"We must make our existence matter and always fight to exist for as long as we can," Jennifer said.

"I know I am old, but I am too young to die, but I can`t live with all this pain," Jackson whispered.

"Of course you are too young to die and the pain is only temporary. You have lots of years ahead of you and one day we will remember this day as a day that made us stronger and closer to our own convictions. Your destiny is to share your life with Dianne, David and Mary. Your existence enriches your family's existence. You have every right to live as if you are the boss. That is what Mr. Coaltonstone does. His life is his own. And he answers to no one. It is the same with President Peel. He shuts down what he wants, when he wants and doesn't answer to anyone," Jennifer said.

"Where are the medics? Why can't someone help us?" Dianne screamed. "Is that Dr. Smith? He is walking towards us, thank God," Di said as she tried to wave to him but she was too weak.

"I think that is President Peel following him," Jennifer noted.

"Sir you can't just park a helicopter on wild flowers that have taken so long to bloom," President Peel shouted.

"That man is proof that there are still good people out there in the world and what they do still matters. Dr. Daniel Smith doesn't always believe in everything we believe in, but he has always believed in our right to say it," Dianne said.

"I see that President Peel is shouting at him. He shouts at everyone," Jennifer said.

"Sir, I told to move that helicopter at once, you are crushing the flowers and disrupting my rally and the wind is messing up my hair," President Peel said.

"Well you are not my president, I would have voted for James Coaltonstone if I had been old enough. You bully everyone who doesn't bow down to you. This doctor is risking his life to save Dianne Black and Jackson Black from bleeding to death. All you promote is love for money, at a time when you are living proof that money can't buy happiness," President Peel said.

"Mr. Peel, I am a first responder in a medical emergency, which gives me authority to do what I see fit, to save these two reporters' lives. And yes, your bald spot is showing, so what? Everyone knows that you have one. I crushed a few wild poppies, so what? The fact you are oblivious to the pain and suffering of others makes you unfit to be president. And I agree with this brave young lady, one of the bravest that I have ever see, you are not my president, either," Doctor Smith said.

"Hello Dianne, You look ravishing as ever, but that Jackson over there looks awful," Doctor Smith said.

"It is impossible to compete against Dianne in the beauty department, especially when your bowel is partly hanging out of your gut," Jackson said.

"I saw the stabbing on TV," Doctor Smith explained. "James Coaltonstone phoned me and requested my existence. James was right. There are no medics and no ambulance. The president is yelling at me because I parked the helicopter on a bunch of wild poppies. I have never seen such chaos. Why are you still lying on this damp ground? Were they just going to let both die while they broadcasted the event live on TV as if it were some reality show? Thank God the knife broke and that maniac wasn't able to do any more damage than he had already done. That is very rare. You two should have been taken to the hospital the moment he was stabbed. James sent one of his black helicopters over to my office, and strangely he already had an ample supply of o negative blood packed with all the equipment that we need to give both of you emergency blood transfusions. So what I will be doing is directing these technicians that came with the helicopter to hook you both up to these lines of O negative blood, which works for most people regardless of blood type. Do you know you your blood type?"

"No, don't have a clue," Dianne said.

"Neither do I," Jackson said.

"Quickly now. We have no time to waste. Hurry with that stretcher. We are running out of time. We must be very careful moving him because we don't know what has been cut inside in Dianne or Jackson's abdomen. Now hold those bags high so we don't get air in the lines. Quickly! Quickly! I must phone and have the hospital at the medical university prepare the operating rooms for two emergency laparotomies. There won't be much room in the helicopter, but we can make room for that young lady if she would like to accompany us to Tut Territory Medical University," Dr. Smith said.

"Sir, I would be very grateful if I could go with Di and Jackson to the University Hospital," Jennifer said.

"What are all these people doing surrounding Jackson and Dianne like this, please people step back. This is not a circus but a medical emergency, keep holding those bags high, there are hooks to hang them on when we get into the helicopter. And put out all cigarettes and smoking materials," Doctor Smith ordered. "And I mean you too, Mr. Peel."

"You know I never expected or wanted this to happen. This fake news thing, it had nothing to do with me. It just gets people going, and it works so well for President Peel. It is like name calling, we don't mean it. It is just a lot of fun. And it appeals to the prime instincts in people around here," President Peel said.

"Sir, you think this is a lot of fun? Sir you are not fit to be president of this great Republic. If it were up to me, I would certify you. Your bumper sticker rhetoric might be easy for your and your following to remember, but we all know who takes on the personal liability, don't we, Mr. Peel," Doctor Smith said.

CHAPTER 13

In-Reach Entry, LOG #4, written by Dr. Daniel Smith Around 10:15 PM March 21st, 2031

Today has been another inhuman day in the mental decline of the population. And I am not talking about the alleged the Wednesday Night Massacre that was ordered by the authorities on March 19th, late at night, while women and children will sleeping in their beds. We are not allowed to enter the Buzzard Creek Tent City, even though the Red Cross have been demanding permission to enter. One or two pictures of the Buzzard Creek Tent City Massacre that do get out are being called Fake News, by President Peel and this administration.

It is no wonder, Dianne Black and Jackson Green were stabbed, brutally, by one of those maniacs who was attending President Peel's rally. The injuries were horrific but the prognosis is good for both Dianne and Jackson. There was no damage to internal organs though Jackson's bowel had to be pushed back into place, which is how viscous the attack was. It is amazing that the stabbings did not cause more damage than they did.

The physical injury will take about six weeks to two months to heal, but recovering from their mental trauma could take a lot longer maybe they will never recover.

Jennifer Jones, who was not physically hurt, appeared emotionally traumatized. Even though Jennifer was clearly upset by her ordeal she did show compassion and common sense by taking off her own coat and sweater with the good intentions of making Jackson and Dianne feel warmer and more comfortable.

I watched Jennifer's face as Jackson said in a trance like manner while he was being carried to the helicopter, 'avenge this harm by creating your own destiny. Avenge this harm by not creating harm,' whatever that means.

There is something about Jackson that disturbs me. I know he is a brilliant cameraman, and both he and Dianne have ducked hundreds if not thousands of bullets while documenting some of the most dangerous warzones on the planet, but he seems so angry. Jackson doesn't blend in. If I did not know him, I would mistake him for a homeless person, though a very handsome one. And he was willing to let Ginger Goodwin take the blame for Deep Coal's whistle blowing activities. Jackson Green is a man that has a lot of pain, and a lot of anger, and after this brutal stabbing he will have a lot more and hopefully he will be able to control his temper when he needs to.

Both Dianne and Jackson said they wanted to quit covering wars, conflicts and President Peel rallies so they can live a peaceful life, while taking care of their adopted children Mary and David. They also said they want to take up gardening and grow their own vegetables and flowers for their dinner table. I will believe it when I see it. Maria, Mathew Watson's grandmother is the acting live in nanny for the time being, and I would say she has her hands full though Jennifer Jones is helping Maria out a great deal with a lot of the household chores and amusing the children with her etherplayer.

My guess is, once Dianne and Jackson recover from their injuries, they will return to their jobs as news correspondents for the PPZ. I am also certain that they will resort to their old coping skills of denying their fear. I am certain Dianne and Jackson are not ready for retirement and will continue their show and tell news stories from warzones and bloody conflict areas.

Maybe if ordinary people are reminded what it is like to live in war torn countries, they will find better ways to solve conflicts and maybe even show respect and concern for all stakeholders in the equation.

I have been monitoring President Peel without his knowledge. The Brotherhood's board of directors demanded that I include some form of tracking device along with the implant that I installed in President Peel's brain. This implant is designed to enhance the electrical circuitry of President Peel's brain. I am not sure if what I have been asked to do by the Brotherhood is even ethical, actually I am certain that it isn't. I was told that I would be very sorry if I did not comply to their demands, since we are at war and President Peel is the acting commander in chief. The Brotherhood's Board of Directors had concerns that President Peel was becoming a pathological liar, and it might be that he is losing his ability to connect past events into the present moment or it might be just because that is who President Peel has become, a pathological liar. There is something very wrong with President Peel but all tests show that he is of sound mind and body.

I have detected small signs of cause for President Peel's mental decline. A bit of plague tangles and shrinkage, not in astounding amounts, and actually quite normal for a man of his years. My concerns are with his fitness level to be president. My concerns are also shared by the Brotherhood, of course. I have discussed the matter with President Peel and framed that the best prognosis will be trying implant therapy, which is showing positive results as a memory enhancer. Once President Peel understood what the implant could do, he demanded to start the implant therapy right away, 'which stimulates the brain and makes it 'huge', in his own words.

While implanting the brain stimulator device, I also implanted a sensor and movement transmitting device, upon the request of the Brotherhood. I have many concerns about this operation. One is the scar tissue that may accumulate over the years, though President Peel may not have many years left, so I agree with him, that quality of life at the moment, matters more. We just don't know enough about this technology to know whether the benefits are worth the risks, for a younger person. But for a man that is President Peel's age, the benefits most likely do outweigh the risks. Anyway, the brotherhood is not concerned about the risks to President Peel or the risks President Peel is imposing on the rest of us. All that the Brotherhood's Board of Directors seem to care about is the ability to track Mr. Peel's movements and to have optimal storage capacity to store his data activity in their database. It is almost as if the Brotherhood is using President Peel as a puppet for their own agenda, without concern for his welfare.

I am not sure whether President Peel feels anything at all when he places people at risk with his hate speech rallies. He must know that people who don't have a lot going on in their lives, don't know where they will be in ten years' time, and maybe they don't even care. Hate and fatalism have already conquered them. They probably believe that they don't have any say or control in shaping their own destiny. The fanaticism, which could drive a man to stab Jackson and Dianne so brutally, is frightening. It seems that President Peel controls his followers through hatred and the falsification of history. Another concern I have is that some of President Peel's supporters are convinced that they are protecting their president, when they act impulsively and violently towards members of the community who have more liberal values, which are obviously in conflict with their own.

End of In-Reach entry, LOG #4 by Dr. Daniel Smith MD (Tut Island University Hospital).

"Have you completed your log yet, Danny? I have a bit of an emergency. I was hoping that you could carry my heavy bags out of the elevator for me, after you finished writing in your log, but my luggage has disappeared," Edna Smith said frantically.

"Edna, tell me that you are not kidding. You actually left your luggage in the elevator of one of the busiest hotels in Tut Metropolis, waiting for me to finish writing my log, the evening Jackson Green and Dianne Black were stabbed by a maniac at one of President Peel's rallies?" Doctor Daniel Smith asked.

"I only left the luggage in the elevator for a few minutes, dear. Hold on Danny, I need to answer my phone," Ada said.

"That is not your phone ringing, Edna, it is the hotel's phone in our bedroom," Doctor Daniel Smith said.

"Right dear, it is that nice man from the hotel's service desk. Someone noticed that my luggage was riding the elevator alone, and brought my bags to the lost and found area at the service desk. Thank God I had the foresight to put name tags on my bags. Now someone from room service is going to bring my luggage back up. I ordered herb tea and pastries, if that is okay with you, Dear? There are still good people in this world, Danny," Edna Smith said.

"That will be fine, Edna. I am famished. Lucky for your luggage, the world is not full of maniacs and thieves, though it feels that is what the world is destined to become. Hopefully President Peel doesn't get the good people who are left in the world, killed by taking advantage of what he perceives to be their weakness, which is human kindness. Not everyone wants to hone their killer instinct, do they, dear?" Doctor Daniel Smith asked.

"I certainly do not want you to be honing your killer instincts. You would be a lot less loveable and it wouldn't be civilized, though I am sure you would be very effective and dangerous, if the right buttons were pushed. I am sure there are mothers out there, who love those people like a mother always does. Even those who are causing mayhem at Trump's rallies. Who else could really love those deplorables, except their mothers? They were so frightening to watch on TV this afternoon, and they made me ashamed to be a Tutonian. And then stabbing those poor reporters. How can anyone love people like that?" Edna asked.

"It is a shame isn't it? The very people that could use a good hug and a bit of love, are they very people President Peel is convincing that a culture of hate and mindlessness is actually normal," Doctor Daniel Smith said.

"If it were up to President Peel, we would all be shouting at each other," Edna Smith replied.

"I would never shout at you Edna," Doctor Daniel Smith said.

"I saw you shout at President Peel, though. It was on international TV. You looked so handsome and passionate," Edna Smith said.

"We would be nothing without our passions would we

dear?" Doctor Daniel Smith said.

"They are denying that the massacre happened, even though I heard some talk of it at City Hall yesterday. Do you think getting lost in passion is why all this madness is happening and is so catching? Some of the ladies that I was talking to earlier today are refusing to believe that there was a massacre at the Buzzard Creek Tent City, on Wednesday. They believe the event is just another fabrication of what President Peel is calling Fake News," Edna explained.

"I am certain that the Wednesday Night Massacre, happened. The Red Cross have been demanding access to the Buzzard Creek Tent City, so they can see for themselves the condition of the miner colony," Doctor Daniel Smith said.

"I believe that the Wednesday Night Massacre happened too, though I don't want either of us to get involved," Edna replied.

"If I am asked to attend to the sick and the suffering I will. All people matter, not just the rich and powerful. The miners are stakeholders just as much as anyone. I took the Hippocratic Oath, and I intend to live up to those standards. So many people in this administration are afraid of their own insignificance. They are too frightened to stand up and ask for the truth. They seem to think nothing of projecting their bias onto others, in the same that the Exclusion League does. So they think nothing of squashing others, so they can rise in the social order?" Doctor Smith said.

"Well, I am terrified of this administration. All I want is to be left alone to live a long and happy life in peace with you," Edna said.

"Ironic, isn't it? That such madness is being called the New Social Order.

THE END
Stay Tuned for Book Seven

Produced by S.E. McKenzie Productions
First Print Edition September 2019

Copyright © 2019 by S. E. McKenzie
All rights reserved.

Email Address: messidartha@aol.com

www.ingramcontent.com/pod-product-compliance
Lightning Source LLC
Chambersburg PA
CBHW030601130626
46552CB00006B/2627